Lady Jocelyn Courts Blackmail

By

Margaret Bennett

Author's Disclaimer

The contents of this novel are a work of fiction. Any character's name or description is solely coincidental as is any event or incident. Like-wise, the views and opinions expressed in the text do not necessarily represent those of the author. However, any historical errors are either by design or author's error, for which she does sincerely apologize. Mea Culpa.

Copyright © 2021 Margaret Anne Bennett Feuerbacher
All rights reserved.

ISBN: 9798731708623

Other Titles by Margaret Bennett Available on Amazon

Regency Romances

The Earl and the Merchant's Daughter
Foiling the Earl's Affair
The Spinster and the Spy
The Hopeless Hoyden
An Independent Lady
The Impossible Governess
The Poor Relation
A Lady's Dilemma Or The Dandy and Lady Penelope
My Lady Smuggler
The Stowaway Heiress
The Diplomat's Daughter
The Earl and the Vicar's Daughter
Lady Gwendolen, the Long Meg of Berkeley Square

Modern Thriller
Deadly Lessons

Middle School Genre
Jackson's Crew

Visit my website at:
http://margaretbennett.net/

*To Kimberley Elizabeth,
my beautiful, artsy, funny and loving
step-daughter, who courageously and
gracefully faces all of life's challenges.
With love.*

Prologue

Ignoring the prick of his conscience, he tossed back a swallow of brandy.

He'd tried to ingratiate her, woo her, but she'd rebuffed all of his overtures. Nor could he accost her in her own home. Too many old faithful retainers were about to come to her aid.

Now, plans were made and already set into motion.

Even at this advanced hour, White's boasted a fair number of gentlemen playing at cards or having discussions over a bottle of brandy. With his table tucked in the far corner of the room, it appeared no one paid them any heed.

He lowered his voice to a whisper. "You delivered her to King's Place?"

"Yes, the chit's yours for the taking. I've arranged it all with Willa to keep her separate from the other girls."

"Willa will do as you request?"

The other man emitted a malicious low chuckle. "Oh, she'll do as she's told if she wants to keep her pretty neck intact."

"Very well. Did she recognize you?" he pressed.

"The chit never had the chance to see me."

Studying the other man, he took a long pull of his brandy. "When all's done, I'll redeem my vowels."

"About that, you've promised to pay me another thousand pounds over and above what you owe."

"It's as I said. After this night's work, you will get all that and more."

Chapter 1

Spring, 1811
London, England

The door to No. 25 King's Place, located just off Pall Mall with its expensive shops, opened immediately to his knock, granting Adrian George Hylton, the sixth Viscount Stangate, entrance to one of London's newest gaming houses and brothels. "Mrs. Dunlap is expecting you, my lord," the tall and burly major demo said with a bow.

After accepting his cane, hat and gloves, the major demo ushered Adrian into a well-appointed parlor at the front of the townhouse. The resplendent furnishings didn't surprise Adrian. It was what one expected of a brothel located in the *tony* district of Marylebone and catered to its aristocratic clientele.

Upon the door opening, an attractive woman with perhaps four decades in her dish, rose from a cream and gold striped settee and held out both hands to greet him. Hers was a pleasing countenance, and her russet eyebrows and alabaster complexion put lie to her tinted red hair was totally unnatural.

"Lord Stangate, it's always a pleasure to see you," she said in a modulated, cultured tone. Her wide, generous mouth smiled knowingly. "I'm sure Lisette will be equally glad to see you as well."

A sardonic smile split his lips. "Will she?"

"Of course, my lord. Come, I'll take you up, unless you'd prefer to take some refreshment first?" She turned to a cabinet stocked with decanters and crystal tumblers. Her voluptuous figure displayed to advantage in a red, clingy silk gown artfully gathered under her ample bosom while a black embroidered ribbon, that also trimmed the gown's low neckline and offset sleeves, dramatically exposed a risqué expanse of creamy breasts.

"There's brandy in the room?" he asked.

She turned back to him and smiled coyly. "As always, my lord."

"Then I'll go up. I know the way." He bowed over her hand and exited the parlor to cross the hall to mount red carpeted stairs. At the top, he traversed the length of the hall, passing closed doors with different bouquets of flowers skillfully stenciled on each, ignoring the various sounds emanating behind them until he reached a door with a nosegay of violets and opened it.

Entering the bedchamber, he found an attractive young woman sitting in the room's only chair, but who was not Lisette. He frowned. "Have I the wrong room?"

From a heart shaped face, huge pale grey eyes, their luminosity bringing crystals to mind, met his. "No, she-she has another, er, customer," she replied in a weak voice.

He assessed the rich dark brown hair falling about her shoulders in thick waves, the demure scooped neckline of her pale blue gown with a darker blue sash tied under a modishly exposed bosom, the gentle flare of her slender hips, and nodded. She would more than meet his requirements, he decided. "I believe you are in my chair."

Her remarkable eyes opened even wider. "Your chair?"

"Yes, I must to sit to remove my boots."

Fear lurked in her eyes as she stared at him, unblinking.

"If you would allow me to have the chair," he repeated.

"This is your room?" she asked with a frown creasing her forehead.

He chuckled dryly. "In a manner of speaking."

"Oh." She started to stand, but fell back into the ladder-back chair. On a second try, she managed to gain her feet and moved past him to place long slender fingers on top a short bureau, apparently for balance.

Was the chit bosky? He frowned, then breathing in her unexpected, clean lavender scent, he sat in the chair and began removing his boots, all the while assessing her. She appeared young and nervous, almost as if she were an innocent. *An actress,* he decided, *playing the role of an ingénue.* Dispassionately, he ordered, "You may disrobe."

She shook her head, setting her luscious curls in motion. "No."

One eyebrow shot up as he stopped from removing his highly polished Hessian. "No?"

"No. . .my lord." She amended and stood straighter, clasping her hands before her.

He cocked his head to one side. "Is this a game?"

Her small round chin came up. "No, my lord."

"I don't play games," he warned.

"No, my lord," she half whispered.

"Can't you say anything other than 'no, my lord,'" he barked, becoming irritated.

She squared her slender shoulders and bowed her head. "There has been a mistake. I don't belong here."

"Really?" he drawled dangerously.

"Really," she answered this time with a defiant note and raised her gaze, fixing it on something over his left shoulder.

"I'm not amused," he growled softly, his anger rising. He really didn't have time for this tonight.

She reached for the dresser again to steady herself and drew in a sharp breath. "I've no intention of . . . amusing you." She eyed him apprehensively. "Who are you?"

"Who are you?" he shot back.

Many a man had quaked in their boots when Adrian pressed them in that tone. But instead of trembling with fear, the young woman shook her head and tossed her chin up haughtily to declare, "It appears we are at an impasse."

"So it would seem." Despite his anger, his lips twitched at her pluckiness.

"Really, who you are is not important." A speculative glean lit her eyes. "Will you help me get out of here?"

"Why should I?" he asked, thinking how much he'd enjoy running his fingers through her silky, dark brown locks.

"Because I was brought here against my will," she said.

"By whom? The madam?" Willa Dunlap was undoubtedly guilty of many sins, but he had trouble believing she'd stoop to human trafficking. After all, a madam needed girls who'd willingly please her customers.

"Yes—no." She released a sigh. "I don't think she had much choice."

What's this, much choice? "Then who?"

She lowered her eyes to the floor. "I-I can't tell you that."

"Your speech sounds educated." He leaned back in the chair and crossed his arms, expecting to hear a Banbury tale.

"I am." She thrust her shoulders back and stood as proud as any duchess. "I attended Miss Ryder's Seminary for Young Ladies in Halifax, my lord."

"Then what are you doing in this brothel?" His patience was wearing thin. He hadn't time to play boudoir games in a bordello.

"My cousin brought me."

"What?" He'd heard the disgust in her voice.

"Exactly." She lowered her eyes, then raised them, as if she'd come to a decision. "Well, not exactly. I'd ordered my carriage, planning to go to the lending library, when someone hit me over the head. I awoke with my hands tied to the coach's door latch and a blindfold covering my eyes. Then the coach stopped, and a very large and disagreeable man dragged me out of the carriage. He ripped off the blindfold and hauled me upstairs to a room where he locked me in."

She definitely has a flare for drama, he thought. It was a clever story, if a bit bazaar. "Why would your cousin do that?"

Her small chin came up again. "Because I refused to marry him."

Ah, the plot thickens. He smiled knowingly. "So you're an heiress." She compressed her lips together and uttered not a sound. After a few moments, he added, "And now you're compromised and will have to sacrifice yourself at the altar."

She flashed him a cheeky grin. "Oh no, you see I've outsmarted all of them."

"Did you?" Banbury tale or not, like any other male, he appreciated a comely wrench and delighted in watching the changes of this one's facial expressions.

She gave a nervous glance at the door and

lowered her voice. "I crawled out the window."

"Bloody unlikely, we're two stories up," he said skeptically.

She beamed proudly, with a twinkle in her eyes that transformed her from a pretty puss to a stunning beauty. "Yes, but the walls are covered in ivy, enough so I could climb my way over to this window. I did rough up my hands, though," she said looking down at several scratches on her upturned palms.

"You didn't scale the ivy-covered wall to the ground?" he pressed.

She shook her head. "Too many people were milling about the mews, and I couldn't risk someone seeing me. I was lucky to make it to this room undetected."

"Why haven't you tried to escape this room?"

Perfect dark brown eyebrows narrowed over her silver grey eyes. "Someone always seemed to be in the hallway, and I feared being caught. Then a woman came in and told me I had to leave because she needed the room for a-a customer, but—but I sent her away."

Raucous laughter erupted from the hallway, and her eyes darted to the door, then back to him, and she begged him, sotto voce, "Please help me?"

Adrian's suspicions were aroused. "What aren't you telling me?"

She shrugged a shoulder. "I told you Mrs. Dunlap—"

"How is it you know the madam's name?"

"That man was talking to her in the hallway after he locked me in the room." She gave him a questioning look, and he gestured for her to continue. "Well, I told the woman that Mrs. Dunlap sent me here to meet my customer because she was to meet her customer for dinner at Hotel Grillon's." The cheeky smile made another appearance. "I's said as 'ow's Ms. Dunlap said she should wears her best." Her Covent Garden dialect was quite good.

He laughed. "I applaud your inventiveness."

She dipped a curtsey. "Thank you, kind sir."

Studying her thoughtfully, he determined she'd all the markings of a born actress and, with a mental shrug, decided to play her game a little longer. "Be aware, I'm not respectable. Were you found in a bedchamber with me, it would mean ruination for you. For that matter, just being seen in my company could cause it, such is *my* reputation."

She frowned. "That would compromise me?"

He nodded gravely. "Thoroughly."

She was quiet for a moment before her eyes widened. "You'd have to make an honest woman of me."

"But I wouldn't. Afraid I'm an unrepentant scoundrel."

"Oh," she breathed deflatedly.

"Oh," he reiterated, his voice reflecting his resolution.

"That does put me in a pickle," she said, and caught her bottom lip in her teeth.

"Just so." He studied that plump lip, wondering how it would taste, then eyed her attire again. She was dressed like a debutante rather than a barque of frailty, and he mused, if she turned out to be a high flier, he'd consider setting her up as his mistress. She'd certainly kept him entertained—and he still had on his breeches.

She broke into his thoughts. "Have you any suggestions?"

"None."

"You know if you did marry me, we could each just go our own way," she suggested timidly.

"Bloody not happening," he nearly roared, fast losing interest in her tale.

"Not even to save me from my cousin, a fate worse than death," she beseeched him.

"You're not considering my fate," he derided.

"There is that." Her teeth worried that luscious lower lip again, arousing his desire to kiss her insensible.

"There is that," he repeated with a dry chuckle. It felt as if he'd been dropped into a Drury Lane production, a farce no less. Still, her tale was plausible, her speech refined, her dress unexceptionable. Perhaps it was possible . . . . Her remarkable eyes searched his. "Yes?"

"There is another problem." He waited for her to continue as she worried that bottom lip. "I still have to get out of here?"

With nonchalance, he shrugged a shoulder. "Walk out."

"What if someone recognizes me?"

He cocked his head. "Is that likely?"

She considered this for a moment, then shook her head. "Probably not, but I don't believe Mrs. Dunlap will allow me to leave. That's why if you claimed to marry me—"

He shook his head. "I am not marrying you—"

"You'd be saving me from a miserable future," she declared dramatically.

"Would I?" Despite her annoying obsession to see him made a tenant for life, he was enjoying her emoting performance and quite mesmerized by her quivering lower lip. He really would like a taste of her.

"Yes," she devoutly affirmed bringing her hands up to her shapely bosom. "And I promise, we'd never see each other again."

"Nothing could convince me to marry you," he pronounced emphatically, drawing his gaze up from those creamy mounds to meet her eyes.

"I have another plan," she said warming to the idea.

His guard went up again. "What sort of plan?"

She waved her hand about airily. "We could simply pretend."

"Pretend what?"

"Make a show of being betrothed."

He leveled his frowning gaze at her. "Get this through your pretty head. I am not marrying you."

She heaved an exasperated sigh. "Of course not, the whole of it would be a charade."

"This is getting old. Drop it."

She mulishly raised her chin and glared at him. "But don't you see, it's the only way for me to get out of here."

"You can leave with me," he offered, thinking he'd set her up in a hotel until Paddison could rent a house for her.

"But I can't," she gasped. "Besides, Mrs. Dunlap can't afford to let me, either."

What tale was she spinning now? "Are you implying—"

"Yes, she *must* keep me here or else he'll kill her."

"Who?"

"My guardian, of course." A frown marred her smooth forehead. "Or maybe the man who brought me here."

His laugh was sardonic. "What balderdash, though definitely worthy of Drury Lane buffoonery."

"Do you fear nothing?" she asked, incredulously.

He watched her wring her hands for a moment and made the decision to give her the benefit of doubt. He'd been in this room long enough that his ruse might work. If it didn't, well, something else would come to him. "Do you know who I am?"

She shook her head, setting those rich brown curls in motion.

"If I help you escape—"

She folded her hands in prayer. "You'd never see me again."

He nodded. "You'll have to trust me completely."

Her silver grey eyes stared into his for a long moment before she nodded.

"Follow my every lead," he commanded.

He rose and went to a small console where a decanter and two glasses sat. Filling one of the glasses with brandy, he up ended it and drank it down, then gave her a wicked leer and threw his arm over her slim shoulders, pressing some of his weight on her, taking on the persona of a drunkard.

Effortlessly, he slurred, "Come, my love, I've a need to see the Town."

~~~~~

Jossie's nerves tingled at the menacing transformation of the large, broad shouldered man beside her. While sitting down his powerful build posed no threat. But standing next to him with his arm tucking her into his side, she felt dwarfed, even though she was above average in height. "You jest?"

"Never," he swore, dropping his act a mere second and raised a dark brown eyebrow in challenge.

Though his dark features were handsome, a dangerous aura emanated from him, frightening her. Nearly black hair, cropped short and brushed back over a high forehead, set off his cold piercing blue eyes, strong nose, sculptured face with square jaw. The only relief of his impeccably black tailored tailcoat, pantaloons and boots was a silver striped waistcoat and pristine cravat.

Fatalistically, she shrugged. What did she have to lose? He opened the door and, with her pressed against his side, swayed unsteadily out into the deserted hall, headed for the stairs. Reaching the ground floor, he glanced around before starting toward a set of double doors that were open to a large drawing room. Several seating areas, each lit by low burning lamps on inlaid tables, graced the tastefully decorated room.

Toward the rear of the house, she heard a door open, then footsteps coming toward them.

"How could she have gotten out of a locked room?"

Frantic she'd be recognized, Jossie reached up to grab the hand dangling over her shoulder and whispered, "Mrs. Dunlap. That's her."

He nodded and swung her into a small alcove by a window overlooking the street.

"There's no way she could have gotten out," answered the voice of the footman who'd locked her in the room. Jossie tried to twist away, thinking to find a place to hide, maybe behind a settee, when her rescuer's hold tightened on her.

"Trust me," he said softly in her ear, just as Mrs. Dunlap and the footman came abreast of the double doors. His strong arms pulled her into an embrace, and he leaned his head down and kissed her . . . and kissed her . . . and kissed her—passionately!

Almost from the moment their lips met, her fear vanished as a delicious heat suffused her whole being, curling her toes. When she groaned, he deepened the kiss, and her knees weakened, and she all but forgot the perils facing her behind his back.

It was several long moments before he released her to grab her upper arm and half drag her quickly out the drawing room doors and across the now empty hall to a closed door. He opened it, poked his head inside, and pulled her in, closing the door behind them. Still holding her arm, he crossed the room to a set of French doors with dark blue velvet drapes.

Before she knew what he was about, he released her to reach up and grabbed the top of a drape, giving it a vicious yank. The end of drapery rod pulled away from the wall, and he wrestled the velvet material off the rod and tossed it around her shoulders. Then he opened the French door and led her through, again closing it behind them.

They stood on a small veranda, with a low stone wall overlooking a garden. Without any warning, he picked her up and dropped her on the other side of the wall and hopped over it to stand next to her. "Come," he said, this time taking her hand and leading her to the side of the townhouse where a narrow alley led to the street.

Moments later, Jossie found her arm tucked into his, walking briskly to keep up with his long strides down the walkway. She was thankful for the velvet drape as the Spring night air was cold and damp. Looking up at his uncompromising expression, she half whispered, "Do you believe in God?"

"Beg pardon?" His hard gaze met hers.

She smiled shyly. "I know you think me a nuisance."

He grunted.

"I prayed that God would send someone to help me, to get me out of there," she confessed.

"Don't mistake me for a guardian angel," he snarled.

"I won't, but you're here, and you did help me."

He answered her smile with a smirk and shook his head.

They came to the intersection, and he motioned for her to stand quietly until he spotted a passing hackney and hailed it.

"Where to, gov'ner?" the jarvey asked as Jossie's rescuer reached for the coach's door.

By the light of the streetlamp, she saw him raise one eyebrow in inquiry. "If you've no place to go, I can put you up at Grillon's until more permanent arrangements can be made."

Did he just give her a slip on the shoulder? Thinking quickly, she gave the address of a well-known modiste on Park Lane. After he relayed it to the jarvey and opened the door of the coach, she couldn't help asking, "Will I see you again?"

Ruefully, he shook his head. "That isn't part of our deal."

"Sorry, I forgot," she sighed.

"It's unlikely anyway. I doubt we run in the same circles, so we part here." His lips quirked into a wry smile.

"Well, thank you," she said and stood on tiptoe to peck him on the cheek before climbing into the hackney. Taking a seat, she found several coins pressed into her hand.

"To pay the jarvey," he instructed.

"Thank you," she replied, suddenly realizing she didn't know the name of her benefactor. "I-I can never thank you enough."

"No need to, my little actress," he drawled. "Though the denouement has been anticlimactic," he gave her a devilish grin, "it's been a most entertaining evening." With that, he closed the door and ordered the jarvey to drive on.

As the hackney moved off, Jossie resisted the urge to look back. Instead, after it rounded the corner, she tapped on the roof, and when the jarvey slowed the coach, she let down the window and gave him her aunt's address. She daren't go back to her father's London house. Her cousin would be there, and she was bound and determined not to be put in a compromising situation by him ever again.

Chapter 2

"She's not here," Willa Dunlap said, taking a half step back from his murderous glare.

"How is that possible?" he growled. "She was delivered to your very door. All you had to do was keep her confined until—"

"Yes, but you don't understand. The dratted girl managed to switch rooms."

"What do you mean?"

"She was locked in the room next to Lisette, but somehow ended up in Lisette's room, the one that Lord Stangate was sent to."

"Stangate." He grabbed a fist full of her hair with one hand, ignoring her whimpers. "You let Stangate take her?"

"No, no," she pleaded.

He fisted his other hand and struck her face, then shoved her limp body to the floor. Methodically, he pulled down on his waistcoat and shot his shirt cuffs, all the while keeping a malevolent eye on her, daring her to move.

"I better not hear a word of what transpired here tonight," he threatened. Then, he turned on his heel and walked calmly out of the room.

All the next day, luminous silver grey eyes intruded upon Adrian's thoughts. He was distracted from business at hand a number of times, remembering the little actress's impish smile, the clean lavender scent of her when he pulled her into his arms, the fierce hunger to possess her. He kept telling himself no woman could measure up to the image of the minx his mind conjured up.

Logically, there was only one way to correct the alluring memory. So later that night, he acted on his desire and returned to the King's Place, where he was received by Mrs. Dunlap.

"Welcome, my lord." The red-headed abbess slipped her arm through his and led him to the opulent drawing room. It was early yet, and only two other young bloods were enjoying the attention of several of the Cyprians. "I'll have one of the girls tell Lisette you're here."

He accepted a snifter of brandy from a tray offered by a voluptuous older lady, whose generous breasts spilled over the low neckline of a purple velvet gown. "Before you do, I've a delicate matter to put to you. Not to insult the fair Lisette, but I'm here to see the young woman I was with last night."

"I'm afraid she's not here," she replied over the top of her wine glass.

He raised one eyebrow. "Do you expect her to return?"

She hesitated a moment before replying. "No, she, ah, didn't work out."

"Really, I hope it wasn't because of something I did?"

She shrugged one bare shoulder and glanced up at him through her long dark lashes with a knowing smile. "I did see you embracing a lady in the drawing room. I assumed it was her, but then you left rather suddenly."

He ignored the jibe. "Do you know where she went?"

"No." She turned aside, surveying the other occupants in the room.

For the first time, Adrian noticed what looked to be a bruise on the proprietress's cheek, cleverly masked with powder and rouge. "Do you know who she is?"

She glanced back at him and tittered. "Why all the questions, my lord?"

He smelled a rat and lost patience. "Cut line, Willa. Someone brought the girl here. Who was it?"

The color drained from her rouged cheeks, making the bruise on her cheek stand out, and a flash of fear appeared in her eyes. But she recovered quickly. "That I cannot tell you, my lord."

He gave a small sarcastic chuckle. "What's this, honor among thieves, or such?"

"More like I've no desire to have my throat slit," she said barely above a whisper, dread reflected in her eyes.

He'd worked among London's criminal elements long enough to recognize the fruitlessness of trying to pull from her the name of someone whom she feared more than himself. He'd need to explore another avenue to get answers.

He drained the remains of the brandy snifter. "Is Lisette available?"

She was, but though he posed similar questions to her, it appeared she knew next to nothing.

"That little hussy sent me on a fool's errand to Hotel Grillon's," Lisette complained while coyly batting her eyelashes at him and slowly tracing the embroidered pattern on his waistcoat.

He smiled to himself. He still suspected last night's cheeky minx was an actress, though he couldn't guess what her game had been other than a farcical charade possibly concocted by some harebrained young bloods.

Before leaving, he apologized to Lisette for the previous night's mix up and handsomely compensated her for the inconvenience.

Perhaps he'd swing by the theaters later that night.

~~~~~

Two days later after her ordeal in the brothel, Jossie was safely ensconced in Lady Cassandra Welbeck's townhouse on Mount Street. As she looked across the rim of her tea cup at her aunt, she wondered how much the older woman resembled her mother. In her mid-fifties, her mother's elder sister possessed blue eyes, a slightly longish nose, dark eyebrows set in an attractive face with few wrinkles, framed with a glorious crown of silver white hair.

"You're not attending me, Jossie," Aunt

Cassie said, reaching over to pat her knee. Dressed stylishly in a long-sleeved, cerulean blue muslin gown with frills of Vandyke lace at the high neck, she still possessed a comely figure.

Jossie shook her head. "Forgive me for woolgathering."

"Of course, dear, but I was saying it'll be so nice having someone to share the Season's entertainments, now that you're staying with me."

Since she'd spent most of her life either at her father's main seat, Allenby Park in Yorkshire, or at Miss Ryder's Seminary for Young Ladies located in Halifax, this idea definitely appealed to Jossie. She'd made her come-out with her stepmother two years ago, but had returned to the Allenby Park and remained there due to the duchess's confinement for a disappointing third daughter, and hadn't returned to London until recently.

Jossie beamed. "I would like that."

"Very well, and who knows, we might just find you a husband."

"Of my own choosing, Aunt Cassie?"

"Yes, my dear, one of your own choosing."

Jossie met her aunt's smile with another of her own.

"Now, it's early days of the Season yet, and London is thin of company, which will give us time to order a few new gowns. Lady Kedleston is hosting a ball for her daughter's come out a week this Saturday, and I plan to attend."

Jossie was prevented from replying when her ladyship's butler, a small man with a balding pate of iron grey hair and a pugnacious nose, announced, "Mr. Rupert Malton, my lady."

Lady Welbeck sighed and said to Jossie, "How tiresome, but of course we cannot turn him away." To the butler, she said, "You may show him in, Dilhorne."

Moments later, the Duke's heir stood bowing over her aunt's bejeweled hand. He was average in height with thinning light brown hair brushed forward a la Brutus with long sideburns. "Thank you for receiving me, Lady Welbeck," he said, then turned walnut brown eyes to Jossie and looked down his long aquiline nose at her. "Cousin Jocelyn, quite a fright it gave me when you disappeared from Manchester Square the other day without so much as a word or note."

When she offered no explanation, he added haughtily, "Then to add insult to injury, the next day your lady's maid packed your trunks and brought them here. Such behavior is most unbecoming, Cousin. You must return home."

Jossie straightened her spine and glared at him. "I've other plans."

Before he could reply, Lady Welbeck spoke up. "You may style yourself as Jocelyn's guardian in Town, Rupert, but you've no authority to tell her what she can or cannot do."

"I'm sure the Duke would want his daughter residing in his own townhome," he retorted with a sneer.

"I've already written to Allenby," her ladyship said, "and explained that as you are a bachelor residing in Manchester Square, it's unacceptable for Jocelyn to stay there without proper chaperonage."

"What nonsense," he growled, his face flushed with anger. "She's my first cousin."

Lady Welbeck nodded. "Which brings me to your reprehensible behavior."

"My behavior," he nearly howled.

Her aunt's sharp gaze narrowed. "Doing it much too brown, Rupert. As her protector, it was despicable of you to take advantage of the situation and force your advances on her."

"That's absurd," he objected, tossing a menacing glance toward Jossie.

"Jossie's told me everything." Lady Welbeck's words sounded like a death knell. "I shudder to think what His Grace would say about your actions."

"Is that what you wrote to him?" His breathing had quickened and a sheen of perspiration dampened his forehead.

"No, for such deportment is best forgotten and buried for everyone's wellbeing."

He let out a long breath. "This is nothing but a misunderstanding. I don't know why Jocelyn would tell you such lies—"

Lady Welbeck held up a slim bejeweled hand. "Don't try my patience, Rupert, or His Grace will definitely learn the whole. Now, be off. I'm quite put out with you."

As if on cue, Dilhorne opened the drawing room door and stepped inside. Rupert threw a savage glance at the butler, then Jossie. "Very well," he said through gritted teeth. "I bid you good day, my lady, Cousin." Turning on his heel, he brushed past the rigidly erect Dilhorne, who bowed to his mistress before following behind him.

The ladies sat in silence, hearing Rupert's heavy footsteps on the stairs, and seconds later the slamming of the front door.

Aunt Cassie looked at Jossie with a raised eyebrow. "I do believe that went rather well, don't you, my dear?"

Feeling as if a heavy weight had been lifted off her, Jossie's smile grew until a merry laugh peeled out of her.

Chapter 3

Well over a week had passed since the chance meeting with the engaging actress at twenty-five King's Place, and still Adrian couldn't get the minx out of his mind. He was haunted with memories of her unusual eyes, her delectable figure hinted at under a demure debutante's gown, her inventiveness to weave a plausible tale. Bloody hell, the chit's image not only cut up his dreams but his waking thoughts as well, and he didn't even know her name.

He'd more than enjoyed their kiss, the feel of her soft curves under his hands as he'd embraced her, and hoped to see the beauty again to further a relationship. It was rare a female got under his skin, and he'd acknowledged that if he found her, he'd set her up as his convenient, a most uncommon practice for him.

So driving down Park Lane, on impulse Adrian pulled his curricle to the side of the road at the address he'd heard the actress give to the jarvey that night. He wasn't surprised to find it was a modiste's establishment instead of a residence as he tossed the reins of his matched chestnuts to Loughry, his groom. Entering the shop, he asked for the modiste and inquired if any of her clients fit the actress's description, but to no avail.

So he began making the rounds of the Green Rooms at the various theaters, and still failed to catch a glimpse of her. It appeared the little minx had vanished like a mystical fairy.

In between times, he went about his duty with the Home Office, prowling the gentlemen's clubs, trying to ferret out information about a suspected traitor. He also kept his ear bent for any on dits about a missing young lady or compromised heiress, and as he heard none, concluded his supposition that she'd been a talented actress was correct.

Then presently, another, more pressing and personal problem confronted him.

Two months ago, at the Marquess of Lyttelton's benefit masquerade for the foundling hospital, he'd met a young widow, or so she'd claimed. She had given her name as Beatrice Winslow and said she was in Town visiting friends. He was instantly attracted to her, and pursued her most of the evening. At the masquerade's conclusion, he took her to Grillon's, ordered a light repast and wine before securing a room and experiencing a delightful interlude with the lovely Mrs. Winslow.

Thus over the next few weeks, they enjoyed each other's company several times at the hotel, until he received her first billet-doux and immediately severed the relationship. To date, he'd received two more, each more maudlin than the last. She could hound him all she wanted, but for Adrian, the affair was finished.

Then tonight, after attending a British Embassy dinner for the Belgium ambassador, he'd dropped in on Lady Kedleston's ball. He'd just congratulated his hostess on having the first crush of the Season, when George Lindell, the Earl of Bolton, an acquaintance of his that he knew from working at Whitehall, greeted him with Beatrice Winslow on his arm.

"Lord Stangate, allow me to introduce my wife, Lady Bolton," Bolton said and bestowed a proud smile on Beatrice. "Beatrice, this is Adrian Hylton, Viscount Stangate."

Bloody hell! It took all of Adrian's training to control his roiling anger. He'd been duped into breaking one of his cardinal rules—no dalliances with society's debs fresh out of the schoolroom, other single eligible ladies, or another man's wife. Keeping his face expressionless, he met her gaze and bowed his over her hand. "A pleasure, Lady Bolton."

Her eyes seemed to be pleading with his as she gave him a tremulous smile. "Thank you, my lord."

"You'll excuse me," Adrian said, "but I see Lady Jersey over there and must say hello."

"Perhaps one of these days, we'll meet at White's, share a bottle together," Bolton said, before guiding his wife onto the dance floor for a quadrille starting up.

Adrian took a glass of wine off a tray that a passing footman carried, upended it, and drained the contents, then skirted the edge of the room to join Lady Jersey. That needle-witted patroness of Almack's saw him coming and turned from the other ladies she'd been chatting with to tap his black superfine sleeve with her closed fan. "This is an unusual venue for you, Stangate."

"Kedleston cornered me at White's. Asked me to put in an appearance for his daughter's come out."

Sally Jersey laughed. "Dare I hope, after this, we'll see you at Almack's?"

"One never knows," he said, though his tone suggested otherwise. His eyes caught a dark haired young woman going through the movements of the quadrille with a besotted sprig. When she raised large, luminous, silver grey eyes to her partner, his heart stuttered. "Do you know who the fair damsel is on young Carlisle's arm?"

"You don't know?" Lady Jersey chuckled. "That is the Duke of Allenby's daughter."

Adrian eyebrows elevated in surprise. "A by-blow at Amelia Kedleston's ball?"

"Hardly." She scoffed and eyed him speculatively. "The lone surviving progeny of His Grace's first wife, the former Lady Mary Fortescue."

"Ah, she died in childbirth?" His mind whirled as he realized his minx of an actress was, in fact, an heiress and the daughter of a duke. Apparently, her little tale was true.

Thus erasing any future plans he'd had to

make the bewitching minx his mistress.

"Exactly, the second duchess has very little to do with her stepdaughter."

He smiled sarcastically. "Never suggest Her Grace personifies the wicked step-mother."

"Just so, and a jealous snake when it comes to Lady Jocelyn," she said, nodding her head. "Of course, in the Duchess's defense, it must be difficult bringing out a gel who is a mere five years younger than yourself and twice as pretty."

"Why haven't I seen her before?"

"Perhaps if you'd attend *tonnish* entertainments more often?" She gave him a knowing smile. "Then too, Allenby wants a male heir and has kept Her Grace *enceinte*. Poor Nora has given him three girls already, you know," she said as an aside. "The Duchess is in a delicate way once again and seems content to remain in Yorkshire, but she shuns Lady Jocelyn's company. Seems her aunt, Lady Welbeck, has recently stepped up and taken the gel on for the Season."

For several moments, he silently watched the young woman, well aware of the Almack's patroness's keen scrutiny of him as he did so. As the quadrille came to an end, he said, "I beg an introduction, my lady."

"Of course, Stangate," she replied with a trilling laugh and took the offer of his arm to lead her over to where Lady Welbeck sat with several other matrons observing the dancers.

As Lady Jocelyn's escort led her off the dance floor, Adrian observed her graceful stride. She presented a stunning picture in a cream colored satin gown with a blond lace overskirt edged in sliver and caught up under her modestly exposed breasts with a sliver sash. As the couple neared Lady Welbeck's side, her luminous eyes widened, betraying her recognition of him, and he chuckled to himself. By Jove, he couldn't wait to hear what tale she'd spin now that she was caught out.

Sally Jersey introduced Adrian first to Lady Welbeck, then to Lady Jocelyn. With introductions aside, he asked for her hand for the next dance.

"I'm sorry, my lord," she said, appearing not one whit so, "this dance is bespoken already."

"George Burghley, isn't it," Adrian hailed the young gentleman approaching.

He nodded his head. "Lord Stangate, a pleasure."

Adrian gave the young man an unapologetic smile. "Afraid you might not see it that way, as I'm usurping your right for Lady Jocelyn's hand for this dance."

"See here, Stangate, that's not well done of you," Burghley complained, but good-naturedly. Then he turned to Lady Jocelyn and requested another dance before he left.

As the strands of a waltz started up, Adrian led Jocelyn on to the dance floor and, drawing her unseemly close to him, reveled in the feel of her slim waist where his hand rested at the small of her back. He smiled down at her. "So your father is the Duke of Allenby. Is he the evil villain of your story?"

Her glorious silver grey eyes met his. "His Grace has never been unkind to me."

Curiosity got the better of him. "Then you've told him what happened?"

With a look of dread, she reared back into his embrace. "Good heavens, no. Why, I can just imagine what he'd do."

Adrian's own expression sobered. "More than likely, His Grace would see me hung if he became aware of my part in it."

"Knowing my father, I rather think he'd see you marched to the alter—at gun point. A fate worse than death to milord, if memory serves me correctly." The saucy smile she flashed him tripped his heart for several beats. "I believe I owe you a debt of gratitude for refusing to marry me, my lord."

He laughed. "Ah, you've deduced my unscrupulous character. Even so, call me Adrian, Jocelyn."

"I can't do that, and neither can you call me by my Christian name," she protested.

"Why not?"

She coyly lifted her eyes up to peer at him through long dark eyelashes. "We've just met, my lord. It would be most improper," she teased.

He considered her words and nodded. "Perhaps to polite society, yet we share an unconventional history." She shook her head and parted those luscious lips to speak. He cut her off. "A compromise, then."

She giggled. "Do you intend to offer me a slip on the shoulder, my lord?"

He let the desire he felt for her show in his eyes. "Though you've twisted my meaning, honestly compels me to admit I would if I didn't fear the Duke." A rosy blush colored her cheeks, and he smiled before changing course to less dangerous channels. "What I propose, Jocelyn, is when it is only you and I, you address me as Adrian."

"Jossie," she said, "my friends call me Jossie."

"Jossie," he repeated, and decided it fit her. He whirled her around the room, reveling in the feel of her in his arms, inhaling her lavender scent, and wondered what it was about the minx he found so intoxicating. He'd known more attractive and sophisticated women, worldly women who knew how to entertain a man. Jossie possessed polish, yet exhibited an openness, an honesty most women of his acquaintance lacked. Most likely, with familiarity, the novelty of it would wear off.

Still, he didn't want to release her. "You never told me who was the villain of your story?"

Her eyes slid to look at something—or someone over his shoulder. "But I did, my cousin."

"Who would that be?" he pressed. Rather than answer, she clamped her luscious lips together and continued to stare over his shoulder, but he figured he could discover who the miscreant was easily enough. Perhaps put the fear of God in him. "One more thing, should you ever find yourself in need of help, call on me."

She searched his eyes and nodded. "Thank

you, but it will never happen again."

He felt the force of her words like a kick to his heart and intended to question her surety when the music stopped. She curtseyed, then walked off the dance floor, leaving him standing alone. As he watched the seductive sway of her hips, an odd feeling of desolation settled in his chest.

Chapter 4

Though Jossie had never met anyone like Stangate, she resisted the urge to look over her shoulder at him. He was arrogant and overbearing, but waltzing with his strong arm about her waist, his piecing blue gaze fixed on her, had felt exhilarating. Almost as exhilarating as the kiss they shared at the brothel, one that she still dreamed about.

Instead, she returned to her aunt and was soon swept back onto the floor for another dance. The evening flew by, but at one point her heart fluttered when during a cotillion she and her partner were paired with Stangate and an elegant woman who was extremely attractive and closer to the Viscount's age.

Covertly, Jossie eyed the lady. Her light brown hair was pulled up in a loose knot with diamond pins sparkling in the light of the ballroom's two enormous chandeliers. Throughout the dance movements, her honey brown eyes anxiously sought the Viscount's, who, for his part, appeared attentive to the lady while maintaining a cold aloofness. He spoke little to anyone, bordering on rudeness, causing Jossie to wonder why he had bothered to ask the woman to dance.

By the time supper was announced, the overheated ballroom had brought on a headache, and Jossie excused herself from her aunt's side. But instead of the retiring room, she headed for the wall of French doors that opened onto a stone veranda running the length of the back of the house. The garden was bathed in soft light by small candle lanterns hanging from the trees and bushes that extended back to the mews. Picking up the skirt of her gown, Jossie tripped down the flagstone steps and followed a gravel pathway that meandered among low box hedges surrounding an array of late spring and summer flowering plants.

Coming upon the rear gate, she heard the sound of muffled sobs and walked toward the corner of the garden. There under a tree sat a woman on a wrought iron bench, her head down, crying softly into a linen handkerchief. "May I help you, madam? You seem distressed."

When the woman raised her head, Jossie recognized her as the lady who'd been dancing with Stangate. "Distressed?" Her mouth stretched in a wide, tremulous smile from which spilled a hysterical laugh. "What a novel way to describe my demise."

"I beg pardon if I'm intruding," Jossie said, not quite knowing how to react to such a sentiment, and started to move away.

The woman waved her handkerchief in the air. "Pay me no mind," she said before dabbing ineffectually at the tears streaming down her face.

Deciding to do just the opposite in the face of such misery, Jossie sat down beside her. "Please forgive my forwardness, but I wish to help."

The woman, who was probably six or seven years senior to Jossie, looked closely at her. "You're the Duke of Allenby's daughter?"

Jossie nodded. "Lady Jocelyn Graydon."

"I'm Beatrice Lindell, Lady Bolton." Staring off into the distance, she shook her head and seemed to come to herself. "I saw you two seasons ago with your stepmother. She wasn't at all pleased presenting you, if I remember correctly." When Jossie didn't reply, she added with a wry smile, "She fobbed you off on any gentleman who could stand unaided on both legs." Her laugh this time was sardonic. "There didn't appear to be much motherly love on her part."

Jossie cleared her throat. "There isn't, and that's what has brought me to Town."

"So perhaps you might understand," she began hesitatingly, "if I declare I'm in desperate need of a friend?"

"Yes, for I, too, lack any true friends," Jossie said with an encouraging smile.

Lady Bolton studied Jossie for a long moment. "If I tell you something, you must swear never to tell another soul."

Jossie frowned. "I give you my word."

"There's no one else I can turn to, you see."

"I won't betray your trust," Jossie replied taking the other woman's cold hand in her own. "I've secrets of my own I'd like to share with someone."

"I fear my secrets are my undoing." Lady Bolton closed her eyes and whispered, "I have been so very foolish and now face losing everything I hold dear."

Shocked by such anguish, Jossie squeezed her hand reassuringly. "Please, Lady Bolton, I may be young, but I've . . . not had an easy life. I'm also quite resourceful."

"Someone is blackmailing me," Lady Bolton blurted out baldly.

Jossie inhaled and held her breath, waiting for more, but silence hung in the air between them. Finally, she exhaled and said, "Then you definitely need my help."

Lady Bolton pulled her hand free and began twisting the linen square about her fingers. "I will be ruined, my reputation shredded beyond rags."

"Perhaps, but if you share your troubles with me—Well, two heads are always better than one," she reasoned. "First, please call me Jossie."

She gave Jossie a sad smile. "Beatrice."

"Very well, Beatrice, suppose you tell me why you are being blackmailed," Jossie ventured.

More tears pooled in Beatrice's eyes. "I foolishly allowed myself to be taken in by . . . a certain gentleman's handsome countenance and smooth tongue, and . . . before I knew it, I slept with him."

"Oh," Jossie said, then bit her lower lip.

"Oh, indeed," Beatrice replied with a humorless laugh. "It gets worse."

"Worse?" Jossie whispered incredulously.

"I-I became infatuated with him."

"Oh dear."

Beatrice bowed her head and stared at her hands twisting the handkerchief. "I even wrote him a love letter."

"No," Jossie breathed as enlightenment of Beatrice's predicament dawned.

"Yes." She raised her head and stared toward the back of the townhouse. "He took to avoiding me and, foolishly, I wrote two more letters." She turned on the bench to face Jossie. "You see, I'd given him a false name the night we met, so he didn't know me as Lady Bolton, or that I was married. I pretended to be a widow." She drew the twisted linen square to her lips. "He is here tonight and met my husband, who introduced me to him. You see, they know each other."

"What happened?" Jossie asked, completely caught up in the drama.

A sob escaped Beatrice. "He all but gave me the cut direct."

"Oh dear."

Beatrice's eyes took on a haunted look. "I feared he'd say something to my husband. It wasn't well done of me, but he was standing among a group, and I implied that he'd promised the next dance with me." She gripped Jossie's hand. "Jossie, I begged him to say nothing to anyone and to return my letters."

"What did he say?" she asked.

"That's just it. He never uttered a word. He barely looked at me, and when he did, his stare was piercingly cold."

"Do you think he intends to reveal all to your husband?" Jossie asked.

"I don't know." She slowly shook her head. "Shortly after the dance, a footman handed me a note that instructed me to compile a certain list of names." She reached in her reticule and pulled out a crumpled missive.

Jossie took the note, unfolded it and read the dark bold script. *If you don't want your husband to know about the affair you carried on at the Hotel Grillon's, bring a copy of the names and locations found in the documents he brings home. You have two weeks. I'll be in contact.*

Clutching her hands together in her lap, Beatrice drew a shaky breath. "You see, my husband works at Whitehall for the Home Office and has access to sensitive information. If I don't do as the blackmailer asks, he'll expose my . . . indiscretion to my husband."

"Do you have any idea who this—this black-hearted scoundrel is?" she asked. With a sinking feeling in her stomach, Jossie suspected she already knew the identity of Beatrice's tormentor. In her mind's eye, she saw Beatrice's beseeching glances at Stangate who was barely civil toward her on the dance floor.

Beatrice shook her head. "I dare not say. If I can just get my letters back, then he'll have no evidence. It will be his word against mine."

She reached for Jossie's hand, and her grip

tightened almost painfully. "Do you know, the irony of this whole dreadful affair is that I have come to realize how much I value my husband, how much I *love* him."

"Oh," Jossie sighed, her heart touched by the woman's confession.

"I must get those letters back," Beatrice averred. "If Bolton reads them— Well, he'll banish me to the wilds of his Scottish hunting box. Besides that, I cannot—will not commit a treasonous act." She released her hold on Jossie's hands. "So you see, my case is hopeless."

"Beatrice, I cannot help you unless you tell me who has your letters," Jossie reasoned.

Beatrice shook her head. "I fear the man is unscrupulous."

"Yes, but there must be some way to retrieve your letters," Jossie insisted. "Who is the gentleman?"

"Promise you'll not breathe a word of this to anyone?" Beatrice demanded in a tight voice.

Jossie held up her right hand. "I swear."

"Lord Stangate."

"I knew it!" Jossie nearly yelled coming to her feet. "Why that two-faced, unprincipled reprobate, that detestable—"

"Jossie, please." Beatrice hopped up beside her. "You must not bring attention to us. And you must promise, you'll say nothing to him."

Inhaling deeply, Jossie tried to control her ire, and one look at Beatrice's stricken expression was enough to dampen it. She heaved a resigned sigh. "I won't utter a word to anyone, including my Lord Stangate." She bit her lip in thought, then asked, "When are you to deliver the list of names?"

"I assume two weeks from today."

"Will that give you time to get it together?" Jossie asked.

She shook her head emphatically. "No, I refuse to do as he asks. How can I betray my husband and my country?"

"No, of course you cannot," Jossie said, thinking furiously. "You could make up a false list of names and places."

"But I've no idea what he's looking for, or who. Besides, where would I get them?"

"That does pose a problem," Jossie conceded and considered the matter for some moments. "How about names and places reported in the newspapers. Not well known names, of course, but perhaps the casualties that are listed each day."

"That might work," Beatrice agreed.

"That's that, then." Jossie took the crumpled linen from the woman's stiff fingers and began drying her tears. "You must let me know if you hear anything else from him?" At Beatrice's nod, she took her arm and started toward the ballroom. "Come, we'd better get back inside." Patting Beatrice's hand, she added, "Let me think on the matter of the billet-doux. There must be a way to get them back."

~~~~

His stroll through the garden proved to be so enlightening that he waited just inside the

French doors of the ballroom for her to return. When she entered, he offered his arm and invited her to return to the terrace. "I've a small matter to discuss with you," he added.

With a curious glance, she accepted his invitation. "What could you possibly have to discuss with me?"

"Call it a business transaction of sorts, my dear," he drawled, stirring her toward the shadows close to the house. "What would you be willing to do to keep your husband from learning about our affair?"

She cut her eyes toward him and a frown creased her forehead, then smoothed as a sardonic laugh escaped her. "I've no idea why you'd be so moronic."

"For money, of course."

She shrugged a bared shoulder. "Little good would come of it if you did tell him. I'd simply deny it."

"Your husband might find it difficult to believe you," he said annoyed the stupid woman didn't care a fig for her reputation.

She trilled a laugh. "Jerry has his mistress. He tends to ignore my liaisons as long as I'm discrete."

"You were hardly discrete meeting with Chadrick Morley just now," he challenged.

"I'll wager no one other than you saw us." She shrugged one creamy shoulder. "Besides, like I said, it's my word against yours. You can prove nothing. I've no identifying blemishes like Beatrice Bolton. The poor dear confessed to me that she has the most unfortunate birthmark about her navel."

Chapter 5

Other than attending St. George's in Hanover Square for church services, Sunday was uneventful for the ladies in Mount Street. On Monday, however, Jossie accompanied Aunt Cassie to the Theatre Royal in Drury Lane to see Sheridan's comedy *The School for Scandal*.

As luck would have it, Rupert Malton was with several bucks down in the pit and saw Jossie as she took a seat in her aunt's box. Minutes later, a knock sounded on the door, and he entered with another gentleman in tow.

After greeting Lady Welbeck, he turned to Jossie. "Well met, Cuz." He gestured toward his friend. "Jossie, this is Sir Percy Carew. Sir Percy, my cousin, Lady Jocelyn Graydon."

Carew bowed, and while pleasantries were exchanged, Jossie felt defiled as his dark, narrowed eyes lasciviously scanned her from head to toe. He was of medium height and build, with a long face, a round, weak chin and small mouth. His curly brown hair was brushed forward, drawing attention to the permanent crease between his eyes. Overall, his countenance was one of concentrated severity.

Since Lady Welbeck pointedly omitted to extend an invitation for Rupert to join them, he and Carew finally returned to the pit when the curtain rose. As the actors took their places for the opening act, a commotion in a box on the other side of the theater caught Jossie's attention. Stangate had entered it with an attractive brunette on his arm.

Dressed in the height of fashion, her crimson gown trimmed with gold frogging clung to a curvaceous body. The Viscount saw her seated, then leaned over her shoulder to hear something the dark haired beauty said, his eyes focused on her indecently low bodice. Then they rose from the woman's generous décolleté and met hers on the other side of the theater, Jossie felt the intensity of his gaze. A blush burned her cheeks for being caught staring, and she determinedly fixed her eyes on the stage where they remained for the first half of the play.

Before the curtain lowered for the start of intermission, Stangate entered their box and presented himself to Lady Welbeck, then bowed over Jossie's hand. She glanced across the theater to see the dazzler surrounded by several men, all vying for her attention. Meeting Stangate's piercing blue eyes, she asked, "Should you be ignoring your lady?"

"Olivia can take care of herself," he said dismissively and smiled at her, his gaze softening.

"Do you attend the Rennells' soirée on Thursday?"

She nodded. "I believe my aunt received an invitation."

At this point, they were interrupted by the return of Rupert and Sir Percy. Jossie made the introductions, and Stangate appeared none too pleased as he acknowledged each with a nod and a cold stare. Taking her elbow, he leaned close to her ear and softly said, "Thursday eve, save the waltz for me." He placed a kiss on the back of her hand, bid Lady Welbeck adieu and left.

With a flinty stare, Rupert asked Jossie, "Know Stangate well?"

"We've met socially several times," she said evasively.

They stayed only long enough for Rupert to inform Lady Welbeck he'd come around for tea one afternoon, much to Jossie's annoyance.

As she resumed her seat, Aunt Cassie placed a hand on Jossie's arm. "I feel I should caution you, my dear," she said. "It would not do to align yourself too closely with Stangate. His reputation is most sinister, a libertine even."

"You need not worry, for I'm well aware that his lordship has other interest," Jossie replied, staring across the theater at the Viscount taking his seat beside the dark haired beauty. "Do you know who the lady is with him?"

Aunt Cassie's eyebrows pressed together as she peered across the theater. "That is Lady Olivia Alders, and I use the title loosely."

"Is she married?"

"Widowed," she said, her eyes returning to the stage. "Just beware of the Viscount, my dear."

The following morning, Jossie sat drinking tea in the small parlor overlooking the rear garden as her aunt thumbed through a pile of invitations that had arrived in the morning post, discussing which they should accept.

"Lydia Edgeworth is hosting a dinner next week, and while Lord Edgeworth is a dead bore, she usually manages to assemble a most interesting group." Her aunt leaned closer and added, "Edgeworth works for the Home Office and oversees the intelligence agents."

Before Jossie could reply, the butler appeared with a note from Lady Bolton, begging Jossie to meet her later at Hatchard's. "Do you have plans for the afternoon, Aunt? Lady Bolton has requested I meet her at Hatchard's this afternoon." When Lady Welbeck shook her head, Jossie asked Dilhorne, "Is a messenger awaiting reply?"

"Yes, my lady," he answered solemnly.

Rising, Jossie went to an escritoire and drew out parchment, quill and ink. She quickly penned a time when she could be at the bookstore, then handed it to Dilhorne, who left to give it to the messenger.

"You'll take a footman with you?" It was more of a demand than a question.

"I thought to take my maid with me," Jossie replied.

"I'd feel better if you had a footman accompany you," Aunt Cassie said. "Take them both."

Laughing, Jossie said, "No, I'll take Hadley with me."

"Good, he's a strapping fellow, and would have no trouble preventing Rupert from hassling you."

At the stroke of two that afternoon, Jossie entered Hatchard's with Hadley close on her heels and instructed him to wait for her at the front of the bookstore. It took several minutes of roaming the aisles of crowded bookshelves before she came upon Beatrice Bolton near the back of the store.

"You came," Beatrice sighed, lifting troubled eyes from a book she stood holding.

"Of course," Jossie said with an encouraging smile. Walking down the aisle, she joined Beatrice. "Something is amiss?"

Tears welled in Lady Bolton's eyes. "Yes," she whispered, looking around to make sure no one could overhear them. "I received another note this morning. He wants that list now in three days' time."

"You could deny it? After all, it's your word against his," Jossie said pragmatically.

Beatrice shook her head. "What if someone at Grillon's Hotel remembers me? I was there several times. Besides, he said he'll tell George I've slept with other men."

"That's preposterous," Jossie said. "He can't prove such accusations."

"But he can," Beatrice sobbed. "Even

though I'd only ever been with—" She broke off quickly, her eyes darting about, then barely whispered, "You know. Anyway, somehow he knows about a birthmark on my stomach next to my naval and has threatened to use that against me."

"Oh." Jossie frowned.

"George will never believe me," Beatrice wailed softly. She grabbed Jossie's hand. "To make matters worse, George has quit bringing his work home, so there's no way I could copy such a list, even if I hadn't made up my mind not to. Oh, please, Jossie, help me," she pleaded.

"Yes, yes, but how?" Jossie asked bewilderedly. Tears spilled down Beatrice's blanched cheeks as they stared at each other for a long moment.

Beatrice swiped at her tears. "Tell me what to do, Jossie. I can't lose my husband."

"Well . . ." Jossie said as an idea bloomed. "I might have a plan, but I need to think on it. For now, dry your eyes." She waited while the distraught Beatrice managed to control her emotions, then linked an arm through hers and strolled between the tall shelves crammed with books. "Give me today to work out a plan. I'll come by your house tomorrow morning, and we'll discuss what might be done."

It was a fortunate turn of events that Lady Welbeck decided to forgo the Culpepper twins' musical that evening. "For you can be sure," her aunt said, "those gels will monopolize the night. Not that they can't sing—well, at least carry a tune. Will you mind very much, my dear?"

Since this suited Jossie's plans admirably, she eagerly acquiesced, "Not at all, Aunt Cassie."

"Very well, for I dare say it will do us both a good turn to seek our beds early. I'll send a note around telling Lady Culpepper I've a migraine."

Thus, the ladies enjoyed a quiet evening at home, Jossie reading Miss Austen's novel and her aunt embroidering the hem of a linen handkerchief. When Aunt Cassie retired for the night shortly after ten o'clock, Jossie waited barely long enough for the older lady to reach her bedchamber before racing to her own room to put her plan into action. Earlier that afternoon, she'd bribed one of the grooms who lived over the mews behind the townhomes to procure a set of young men's clothing that would fit her. Now, she was anxious to be rid of Becky, her lady's maid, so she could pull the sack they were in from the back of her wardrobe and slip into them.

Her objective was simple, and although she'd been refining it throughout the day, it's success was still riffled with holes. Such as, how could she gain entry into Viscount Stangate's townhouse? Or, where would Stangate keep Beatrice's love letters? She refused even to consider the possibility of getting caught—or the consequences.

Once assured the servants had retired for the night, Jossie discarded her nightrail for the brown coarse cotton breeches, white woolen stockings, dingy muslin shirt, and a rumpled black, wool frienze jacket with large pockets to all of which clung a slight stable odor. Next, she pulled out a pair of scuffed, black leather shoes with buckles, and her nostrils were assailed by their distinctive, pungent aroma. Quickly, she shoved them in the sack and tightly retied the neck. She'd just have to make due with her own boots.

The long clock in the hall chimed the midnight hour as Jossie slipped down the back stairway, tucking her hair under a black knit cap, and exited by the kitchen's back door, then scurried to the rear gate. She practically ran the length of the eerily deserted alley that separated the townhomes from the mews until she reached South Audley Street. Two blocks down, she made a right onto Grosvenor Square.

The Viscount's large corner townhome boasted windows on three sides. Fortunately, because of the lateness of the hour, most of the homes were dark. Still, she scanned the area to make sure no one observed her before she ducked into a narrow alleyway that led from the Square to the mews.

Toward the rear of the townhouse, she squeezed behind a large shrub and rose up on the tips of her toes to peer into a multi-paned window. By the light of a bright half-moon, she espied what appeared to be a study with a large desk to one side and several chairs arranged about it, and two walls lined with shelves. Tucking her fingers under the window's sash, she pushed upward, grunting from the effort—to no avail. The windowpane hadn't budged.

A fatalistic sigh escaped her as she

scrunched down to search the ground for a small rock. It took several minutes, but she found one weighty enough to break a pane without shattering the entire window, which would surely bring servants running, and returned to the window.

With all her might, she took aim and pitched the rock at the middle pane shielding the window latch, fragmenting it nicely. Then using the rock, she brushed aside shards of glass around the edges of the broken pane before plunging her hand through it and unlocking the window.

Now it was a simple matter of lifting the sash, then hoisting herself up on the sill, and dropping down on the floor. She remained crouched by the window, listening intently for any sounds that her burglary had been detected. Hearing none, she rose up and slowly crossed over to the desk, careful to avoid the shards of glass scattered on the floor.

Even with the moonlight streaming in, it was impossible to make out anything on the desk. Turning toward the banked coal fire, she made out the outlines of a lantern on the mantle and beside it a tinderbox. She took a spill from the tinderbox and held it to the smoldering coals to light and applied it to the lantern, keeping the wick low. Going back to the desk, she placed the lantern in the center, noticing a brass candlestick and several paper weights, and methodically began going through the drawers. Several were locked, and in one of those, she suspected, were Lady Bolton's letters.

A pewter letter opener was in the center

draw, and she used that to pry open one of the locked drawers, though not as noiselessly as she'd wished. She was rifling through some papers when she heard a floorboard squeak out in the hallway. Immediately, she extinguished the lantern's wick just as the door flew opened and, grabbing the candlestick, ducked behind the desk.

Heavy footsteps advanced into the room, headed toward the open window, blocking her one means of escape. Recognizing the tall, broad shouldered man as Stangate, a moment's panic gripped her. Jossie knew she had to act quickly before the Viscount discovered her. With his back to her, she rose up, raised the candlestick, and swung it at his head.

There was a sickening clump that made her stomach heave, followed by an obscene expletive as he fell heavily on all fours to the floor. Rushing past him, she made for the window, when his hand grabbed her ankle and viciously pulled her down, slamming her into the floorboards. He threw himself on top of her, forcing the air from her lungs, and raised his fist to strike her.

"No," she managed to croak.

He hesitated before lowering his hand and ripped off her cap.

"You!" he growled, staring at her face exposed by the moonlight shining in through the window. "What in bloody hell are you doing here?" His eyes raked her from head to toe. "Dressed and smelling no better than a stable lad?"

She stared at the sneering countenance hovering over her, his dark features appearing even more demonic in the shadowy moonlight. His eyes resembled hard onyx stones, and mindful of his sinister reputation, she felt a moment of uncertainty, even fear, being alone with this man.

However, she still could barely breathe with his weight on her, for her two hands pushing against his chest were useless. "Please . . . off."

Slowly, he pushed himself up to his feet, then fisted a hand around the lapels of her jacket, and hauled her up. After dragging her to one of the armchairs in front of the desk, he shoved her none too gently into it.

"Stay there." He turned to the fireplace to light a spill from the tinderbox and lit the oil lamp on the desk.

As his fierce gaze turned back to her, she shrank back into a corner of the chair and warily watched him take the matching chair beside her. Gingerly, he fingered the side of his head, all the while his menacing eyes fixed on her. After several moments, he looked at his hand. "At least there's no blood." He glowered at her. "Now, why did you break into my study?"

His tone implied he'd have nothing but the truth. With a trembling hand, she dashed a lock of hair from her eyes and tucked it behind her ear. She drew in a deep breath and considered telling a lie, but the hardness of his glare made her reconsider. Finally she let out a long sigh. "You had an affair with Lady Bolton."

She watched him closely, but his expression gave nothing away. Instead, he sat motionless, his cold piercing eyes focused on her face. "She wrote you three lo—er, letters," she amended. She waited for his acknowledgement. None came. "She wants the letters back."

Wordlessly, he rose from his chair and walked around the desk and sat in the chair behind it. His eyes lowered to the drawers, then darted to hers, and he raised one dark eyebrow. He'd obviously discovered the broken desk drawer. Unbuttoning his waistcoat, he reached into an inside pocket and produced a small key. He unlocked another drawer and fumbled through it before seconds later tossing three foolscap missives on top of the desk.

Standing, Jossie stepped to the front of the desk and, with a shaking hand, picked up the letters. "Thank you, my lord," she said, and turned toward the window.

"This time, oblige me by using the front door."

Jossie looked back to see he'd risen from behind the desk and was making for the study door, which he opened and stood aside waiting for her to exit. His face remained expressionless. She brushed past him out into the hallway, feeling a real sense of danger emanating from him. When his hand grasped her elbow and drew her to a halt, a shudder of fear ran down her spine.

His lips curled in a cruel demonic smile. "Well you should be afraid of me. Now, how did you get here?"

She kept her eyes on the front door. "I walked."

"Then I'll walk you home," he said going ahead of her down the hall toward the entrance. He reached for his hat and gloves resting on a console and placed the curly beaver on his head.

"There's no need," she said, desperately wanting to rid herself of his intimidating presence.

He didn't answer but instead drew her toward the front door, where he retrieved a cane. He ushered her out onto the walkway, drew on his gloves and took her arm. "Which way?"

She gestured toward South Audley Street. "Mount Street."

He nodded and, still holding her arm, set off at a steady pace. Not a word was exchanged in the short time it took to reach the mews behind her aunt's house. At the alleyway, she stopped and, when he looked down at her, said, "I need to go in the back way."

"Lead on," he replied and followed her between the mews and the townhouses.

When they reached the back of her aunt's, she whispered, "This is it, my lord. Thank you." She tried to shake off his hold, but his grip tightened. He turned to face her, took her other hand in his, and brought it to his lips.

The moon overhead shown silvery light on his dark features. Another shiver of apprehension ran down her spine, yet reviewing his actions, she found it hard to believe he meant her harm. She realized that, despite his demonic reputation, she was beginning to trust him.

"Have you any idea of the enticing picture you present?" His voice was low, intoxicating.

"Well no, especially considering your scowling countenance," she said.

A real smile split his lips. "My scowl is directed at the inappropriateness of your attire, not to mention the unappealing aroma wafting from it."

She preened with a matching smile. "I am rather proud of it as some ingenuity was required to secure it. I had to bribe the stable boy to get these clothes." She looked down at her toes. "Although, the boots are mine. There was no way I was going to put my feet in the disgusting shoes he brought."

He chuckled, then turned gruff. "Never again repeat this night's performance, Lady Jocelyn."

She heard the implied threat in his voice and took a step back. Nodding to him, she turned toward the gate, and this time he let her go, but stood watching until she was on the other side of the fence. Slowly, she closed and latched the gate on him.

Chapter 6

After breaking her fast the next morning, with Becky in tow, Jossie set out toward Waverton Street and the Bolton residence, a mere fifteen minute walk away. A slight chill greeted Jossie as she descended the shallow steps of the Welbeck townhouse, and observing grey clouds that hinted at rain later in the day, she wrapped her sage green pelisse more closely about her.

Stopping at the middle of a row of grey stone, four-story townhouses, Jossie applied the knocker to the door which was quickly opened by a rotund butler with a balding pate. She explained her purpose and handed him her card. One busy white eyebrow rose upon reading her name.

"Lady Bolton is expecting you, Lady Graydon," he intoned in a deep voice. After directing her maid to the kitchen region, the butler led Jossie to a small back parlor on the second floor where she found Lady Bolton sitting at a writing desk.

Rising to greet Jossie with outstretched hands, Beatrice barely waited until the butler exited with instructions for a tea tray before she cried, "I've been so worried." She pulled Jossie over to sit with her on a yellow-flowered chintz settee. "Were you able to come up with any ideas?"

Jossie observed her hostess's anxious eyes with purple shadows, proof of a troubled night's sleep. She nodded and reached in her reticule and drew out the billet-doux.

Beatrice gasped, then in hushed tones asked, "My dear Jossie, how is it possible?" She accepted the letters and quickly shuffled through them before she stood up and took them to the hearth where a small fire burned. Opening each one, she scanned it briefly before tossing it on the flickering flames. Nor did she make any move until all three letters were reduced to ashes.

Returning to sit beside Jossie, she asked again, "However did you manage to come by them?"

So Jossie related her foray into the Viscount's study and, subsequently being discovered, explained what she told Stangate, who simply handed the letters over to her.

Beatrice was stunned. "I never would have thought he'd give them up."

"Neither did I," Jossie admitted. "Do you know, nothing was said about blackmail."

"I'm sure he wouldn't incriminate himself so," Beatrice said indignantly. "Why would he implicate himself in something as despicable as stealing government secrets, which would surly end his career, if not put period to his life?"

Jossie took Beatrice's hand. "Beatrice, I've given this a lot of thought, and think you should tell your husband the truth and beg for his mercy. Stangate is a cold, dangerous man. He may yet say something to Lord Bolton."

Tears welled in Beatrice's eyes. "You said he just gave them to you without argument." Jossie nodded. "Then, I believe you have the right of it. I must tell all and beg for George's mercy. Truly, I love him."

Curiosity got the better of Jossie. "Then, why did you do it?

"The affair?" At Jossie's nod, she sniffed back tears and said, "I was jealous. He keeps a mistress, though I don't believe he's seen her recently."

"Perhaps if you discussed it with him—" Jossie said, but broke off. She knew that Beatrice's marriage described the norm for many society marriages. In fact, it was accepted by the *ton*, and wives were expected to turn a blind eye to their spouses' dalliances.

With a defeated expression, Beatrice squeezed Jossie's hand and shook her head. "Just having someone to talk to—you've no idea what a tremendous comfort you've been to me."

There was little else to be said, so a short while later, Jossie bade her good day.

~~~~

The following night, Jossie and her aunt attended a drum given by her aunt's friend, Lady Gertrude Rennell, in Berkeley Square. Her husband, Andrew Kenworthy, the ninth Baron Rennell, kept a respectable stable and was known among the racing set, so the Baroness's gathering was well attended. Thus, Jossie wasn't surprised to see many of her acquiesces, including Lady and Lord Bolton in attendance.

Half way through the evening, Jossie was coming out of the retiring room, where she'd repaired a small rip in the pale pink lacy overlay of her cream silk gown, when Lady Bolton stopped her in the hallway.

"Jossie, I've been looking for you."

"You appear rested," Jossie said, noting the absence of dark circles under Beatrice's eyes. "Does this mean you've spoken with Lord Bolton?"

Beatrice's eyes took on a haunted look. "I've been too cowardly," she confided. "I know you're right, though. I must confess all to George."

"He'll be angry at first." Jossie bit her lip, concentrating on the right words to encourage her friend. "If he cares for you at all, and I believe he does, he's bound to come around. Especially if you explain that you know about his mistress."

"I just need to find the right time. But I sought you out to introduce you to a young woman nearer your age before George and I leave for another party. Her name is Miss Whiddon, and—" Beatrice broke off as Sir Percy Carew walked up to Jossie.

"Ah, Lady Jocelyn, a pleasure to meet you again," Carew said, bowing before her.

"I've got to go," Beatrice whispered to Jossie. "We'll talk later." She was gone before Jossie could reply.

Carew offered Jossie his arm. "Please, allow me to escort you back to the drawing room."

As it would be rude to do otherwise, she reluctantly accepted his arm.

"You enjoyed Sheridan's play at the theater last week?" he asked politely.

"Indeed, I find I prefer comedies over dramas," she said. "We all need a reprieve from the melancholy and malaise that surrounds us."

He seemed surprised by her answer. "Surely as the daughter of a wealthy duke, you remain untouched by the sordid affairs and troubles of the common man?"

He was a friend of Rupert, Jossie reminded herself, and knew whatever she said would likely be repeated to her cousin. Looking at him speculatively, she was slightly unnerved to find him eyeing her in a similar manner. "Neither position nor wealth isolates anyone from the hurts or illnesses of this world." Entering the drawing room, she released his arm and stepped away. "I really must find my aunt. She'll be looking for me."

Jossie didn't wait, but hurried toward a group sitting around a cheery fire where she'd left Lady Welbeck earlier and now found her sharing a settee with their hostess, Lady Rennell. As she drew near the two older ladies, a pretty, diminutive blonde with warm amber eyes set in a heart-shaped face approached Jossie with an older woman following close behind. Shyly, the young woman asked, "Are you Lady Jocelyn Graydon, Lady Bolton's friend?"

When Jossie answered in the affirmative, the young woman curtseyed. "I am Miss Mary Ellen Whiddon. And this is Miss Esther Trundle." After Miss Trundle exchanged greetings with Jossie, Miss Whiddon asked if she could have a private word with her, explaining, "Lady Bolton said you might be able to help me." Her voice was barely above a whisper.

As they moved away from her aunt and Miss Trundle, Jossie smiled. "You are the friend Lady Bolton wanted me to meet?"

Her bow-shaped lips lost their smile. "More like an acquaintance of her ladyship." She glanced quickly about her, then leaned closer to Jossie. "Lady Bolton told me you were able to help with a . . . problem?"

Jossie's interest was instantly piqued. "Do you have a problem also?" she asked incredulously.

A blond curl fell forward from her upswept coiffure as the young woman nodded, and she brushed it behind her ear. "Is there somewhere we may talk?"

"There's a small parlor at the front of the house." Jossie remembered seeing it earlier upon her arrival. After telling Lady Welbeck she'd return presently, Jossie bid Miss Whiddon follow her to the parlor. Closing the door, she studied the young woman, and discovered that her petite stature lent a more youthful air to her, and decided Miss Whiddon was probably two or three years older than she. "What exactly did Lady Bolton tell you, Miss Whiddon?" she asked.

"She explained how you retrieved some very sensitive letters for her," Miss Whiddon replied.

"Why would she do that?" Jossie was amazed that Beatrice Bolton would confess her adultery to another person.

"I should explain that she never described the letters' contents, only that it was imperative she get them back, and you got them for her," Miss Whiddon concluded on a note of admiration.

"If I may be so bold, what exactly is your problem, Miss Whiddon?" Jossie asked, wondering if this young woman was another amorous conquest of Viscount Stangate. Unaccountably, a wave of anger overcame her as she anticipated the young woman's damning words.

A sniffle, then tears flooded Miss Whiddon's eyes. "I'm so embarrassed. I don't' know how to tell you," she said, wringing her hands. "I've been living a lie, and if my fiancé finds out, he will never marry me."

"Oh dear." It sounded perilously close to Beatrice's situation. "Come sit down, Miss Whiddon." Jossie led her to a small settee before an arrangement of armchairs by a banked coal fire and waited for the young woman to take the seat next to her. "It can't be as bad as all that."

"But it is." A loud sob escaped her quivering lips. "You see, I was at Lady Rockingham's ball two nights ago when a servant handed me a note."

Jossie's eyes grew wide in disbelief.

More curls were displaced as Miss Whiddon shook her head despairingly. "Someone is blackmailing me."

A sense of déjà vu possessed Jossie. She took in the innocent appearance of Miss Whiddon's soft blond curls and large amber eyes. Even though, from what she knew, Miss Whiddon didn't fit Stangate's usual type, disappointment and dismay nestled in a corner of her heart. It appeared the Viscount really was a vile lecher.

Several voices were heard in the hall growing louder as each second passed, and Jossie feared their tête-à-tête had ended. She pulled a dainty linen square from her reticule and handed it to Miss Whiddon. "This is not the best place to discuss your problem, Miss Whiddon, for someone may overhear us. For now, let us both return to the ballroom, but do come to Mount Street for tea tomorrow."

Miss Whiddon reached for Jossie's hand. "Then you'll help me?"

"First, I must hear your story," Jossie hedged. "But if there is anything I can do to help you thwart this blackmailer, then you've my promise I will give it my best."

The rest of the evening, Jossie spent watching for Stangate's dark head and broad shoulders, but he never put in an appearance. And why should he? Even though both Lady Bolton and Miss Whiddon were here, this was not his usual social milieu.

The morning was well advanced when Dilhorne presented Miss Whiddon's calling card on a silver salver to Jossie in the cozy back parlor where she sat with her aunt. A few minutes later, Jossie entered the drawing room to find her guest pacing before the fireplace.

Seeing Jossie, she stepped toward her with outstretched hands. "Oh Lady Jocelyn, I do hope you can help me."

"I've ordered tea, so we may have a quiet coze," Jossie said, hoping to put the anxious woman at ease. Leading her to the settee, Jossie asked about her fiancé.

Miss Whiddon's little bow mouth broke into a smile. "Harry, that is, Mr. Harold Powlett is the younger son of Baron Wharton and the dearest gentleman I could ever hope to meet," she gushed. "We met at the start of the Season, and, well, have seen each other almost every day since."

"A love match," Jossie said with her own bright smile.

Miss Whiddon nodded as Dilhorne entered the room, followed by a maid carrying a tea tray that was placed on a table in front of Jossie. She took time to see that her guest was suitably supplied with a cup of tea and a sliver of lemon cake before she asked, "Now, who is blackmailing you?"

"I've no idea," the young woman declared plaintively.

"Then how are you to pay him?"

"I'm to be on the Mall in St. James Park at dusk a week from today with five hundred pounds." She leaned toward Jossie. "Lady Jocelyn, I barely have two guineas to rub together."

Jossie waved her hand airily. "Jossie, please."

"Then you must call me Ellen," returned Miss Whiddon.

"Please forgive me for asking," Jossie began, "but with what is he blackmailing you?"

Tears sprung up in Ellen's amber eyes, and she bowed her head. "Oh dear, it's a long story?"

"A long story?" Jossie couldn't hide her astonishment. From what she knew of Stangate, she was surprised the Lothario maintained a relationship for any length of time. More likely, he kept several on-going at the same time, she mused angrily.

Ellen heaved a weary sigh. "I suppose I should start at the beginning. You see, my birth was illegitimate. I was never told who my father was. My mother was an actress and raised me until I turned six, when she became ill and died. None of her friends at the theatre wanted me, so I was packed off to an orphanage where I remained for three years."

"How dreadful for you," Jossie said, remembering the loss she felt not knowing her own mother.

Ellen shrugged a shoulder philosophically. "Perhaps, but I was fed and clothed, in fact, better than the other girls, for I had a benefactor. When I turned eleven, I was sent to a boarding school, Mrs. Bayle's Seminary for Young Ladies, in Devon, near Exeter, where I was well cared for.

On my eighteenth birthday, I became an instructress for Mrs. Bayle, teaching arithmetic, penmanship, and embroidery."

"You've no idea who your benefactor was?" Jossie asked.

"No, though I did try to find out. As a teacher, I had access to the students' records and found my own file." Ellen paused and stared into the fire. "There was nothing there but my academic records."

"How strange."

Ellen shrugged a shoulder. "Yes, then a family in Harpford, Joseph Whiddon, Baron Aylesbeare, and his wife, applied to Mrs. Bayle for a governess for their older daughter who was to come out in a couple of years. They also had a baby late in life and so wanted someone young." She cast her eyes down to the clenched hands in her lap. "I was only with them for a year."

"What happened?" Jossie was spellbound by Miss Whiddon's tale.

"The whole family perished four months ago from influenza, all in the space of a few weeks." She raised sorrowful eyes and said, "It was quite horrid. Even some of the servants died."

Jossie reached for the young woman's arm. "But thankfully you were spared."

A soft mournful wail escaped her trembling lips. "Yes, and the new heir graciously allowed me a month to find another post, but Mrs. Bayle had no positions open and . . . I could find nothing. That's why I did it."

Contrasting Miss Whiddon's story with her

elegant appearance, Jossie intuitively grasped the other woman's problem. "You stole . . . something of importance."

Biting her lower lip, Ellen nodded. "I was desperate, you understand, so I took on the identity of the older daughter, Mary Ellen Whiddon, and packed a trunk with as many of her gowns and wraps as I could." She gave Jossie a sheepish smile. "She—she was slightly bigger and taller than I, but my needlework is quite fine."

"You stole a woman's identity?" Jossie asked incredulously. Her visitor bowed her head as a shameful blush colored her face, and Jossie asked, "May I ask, what is your real name?"

"Eleanor Addison. That's why I chose to be called Ellen, Mary Ellen's middle name."

Despite her misgiving, Jossie was fascinated by Miss Whiddon, er, Addison. "Miss Addison, Eleanor—"

"Please, call me Ellen," she insisted.

"How did you get to London, Ellen?"

"I had saved up most of my wages. It was enough to pay for a ticket on the stage to London and rent a set of rooms in Kensington." Again, she cast her eyes to her lap and bit her lip. "I-I also stole several small pieces of Mary Ellen's jewelry and a silver mirror, brush and comb set, nothing the new heir might miss, to pawn when I got to Town."

Jossie shook her head at this young woman's derring-do. "Did you consider what would happen if you were found out?"

"I did, but Harpford is a small hamlet and

Aylesbeare Manor quite remote. The nearest town is Exmouth on the coast, you see, and the family all but died out. Lord Joseph had ascended to the Aylesbeare Barony only a short time before I arrived, so I didn't expect anyone to know Mary Ellen, or recognize me as the Aylesbeares' governess." She studied Jossie's face and added, "I'm not an adventuress. It all came about quite by accident. I was left without a reference, making it impossible for me to find another quality position."

"Yes, I do understand that," Jossie conceded. "But then, who is Miss Trundle?"

"Esther is another governess in similar circumstances like mine. Her charges, two young girls, died in the epidemic, which hit the whole area pretty hard, and she was turned off. Because of her age, she's in her fifties, she has been unable to find another position."

"So she agreed to your, er, charade?"

Ellen gave her a weary smile. "Not at first, but I convinced her, explaining what I planned, though not the whole of it." She lowered her eyes to her hands clenching the reticule in her lap. "I didn't tell her where I got my funds, for I knew she'd never go along with—with thievery." Looking up at Jossie, she added, "Esther was also desperate with no family to appeal to, no place to go, and very little money."

"When you met Mr. Powlett, did you consider what the outcome might be?"

"Well no, for you see, I had gone with the family to Exmouth one day, and a young man came up to me and addressed me as Miss Whiddon. Of course, I corrected him, but the incident did stay with me. People often remarked how Mary Ellen and I could pass for sisters."

"Was there anything in the note to indicate what proof the blackmailer has that you're not Miss Whiddon?" Jossie asked.

"No, but I've given this much thought," Ellen said. "He must have a copy of Mary Ellen's obituary from the Exeter newspaper."

Jossie considered this for several moments before she pointed out, "Even if we could put our hands on it, it might not serve. All the blackmailer need do is tell Mr. Powlett about Mary Ellen's death. Then your fiancé could verify the truth of it himself."

"Ohhhh," Ellen moaned in despair. "What am I to do?"

"Well, first you must confess all to Mr. Powlett," Jossie advised warily.

"But I'll lose him," Ellen cried, tears beginning to spill down her cheeks. "And poor Esther, I promised her I'd take her with me when I made a good match."

Observing the distraught young woman, Jossie found herself sympathizing with her situation. "If we could find out who the blackmailer is," she began hesitatingly, "we might be able to get the evidence from him."

"Yes, yes." A sudden gleam of hope sparked in Ellen's amber eyes, then just as quickly dimmed. "But how are we to find that out?"

Jossie bit her lower lip before venturing,

"Perhaps when you met with him to put him off, we could learn his identity. You could tell him you need more time to raise funds."

"That's easy enough," Ellen scoffed. "I don't possess five hundred pounds and have no means of raising it."

"Very well, insist you need more time." An idea struck. "I will also go to the meeting place, but earlier and hide, so when he leaves, I can follow him home. Then we'll decide how to foil him." Jossie leaned back on the settee and crossed her arms, satisfied. At least for now, they had a plan.

Chapter 7

The following night, Jossie and Lady Welbeck attended the Marchioness of Raynham's ball. The evening was sultry, and with the crush of people, the ballroom's doors were open to a wide stone veranda at the back of the house allowing people to take the air.

Before her aunt joined a clutch of her friends and other chaperones, Jossie found her hand being sought by Sir Jeremy Carlisle.

"Was hoping I'd see you here tonight, Lady Jocelyn," the young man said as he led her out on the dance floor. "Haven't seen you since Lady Kedleston's ball."

"My aunt favors attending social events hosted by her friends." Jossie smiled as she added, "They tend to be an older set."

"Must be boring for you?" the young man commiserated.

"Actually, there tends to be a lot of political discussion, which I find most interesting." She gave him a wry smile. "Then too, I have a knack for cards."

He laughed knowingly. "Yes, that would come in handy. Whenever I visit my grandmother, hardly an evening goes by that she don't play cards with her friends. Drags me along with her." The quadrille's movements separated them, but when they came back together, he asked, "Mind if I ask you a question, Lady Jocelyn?" At her nod, his smile turned sheepish. "Ran into Rupert Malton, not too far back."

Jossie was suddenly on the alert. "Rupert is my cousin."

"Just so. He seemed to suggest there might be an understanding between you and he?"

"Most definitely not," she sputtered, trying to rein in her temper. How dare the cad put such rumors about. "We're barely on speaking terms," she added, hoping to squash that piece of claptrap.

Young Carlisle's face broke into a wide grin. "Didn't look to me like you two was cozy. Still, thought I'd better check."

Sensing the young gentleman's interest, Jossie smiled weakly. She liked him well enough, but thought him rather immature and silly. Instead, her mind's eye conjured up a pair of piercing blue eyes set in a harsh countenance, and in the next instant, Jossie's gaze collided with Stangate's, who was squiring Lady Bolton in an another foursome. Beatrice, Jossie noticed, did not appear uneasy, but she wouldn't. Good breeding forbade Beatrice to display any sign of distress in so public a place as a ballroom.

Sometime later in the evening, as Jossie's

dance partner returned her to her aunt, Stangate approached her. "My dance I believe, Lady Jocelyn."

Because of the unusually warm night, Jossie had anticipated sitting out this dance to cool off, and so earlier had scribbled an unintelligible name on her dance card. But she couldn't very well deny the Viscount, especially when her imaginary partner failed to materialize. As graciously as she could, she allowed him to escort her out on the dance floor.

And drat! The orchestra struck up a waltz.

Stangate's hand felt possessive as it rested on the small of her back and drew her into his broad chest, immaculately attired in a black and silver waistcoat and black superfine clawhammer jacket. Placing her hand in his, her eyes were level with his pristine cravat, where a large diamond sparkled among its folds.

He was a superb dancer, and Jossie was surprised by the feeling of breathlessness his closeness gave her, but soon put it down to the dizzying swirls he guided her through. He never spoke a word, though once his piercing eyes managed to capture her gaze, they never left hers. As the silence grew uncomfortable, she finally broke it. "The on dit is you rarely frequent balls of this sort, my lord?"

"I've decided to broaden my acquaintances this Season." His countenance remained an unreadable mask. "Have you made many new acquaintances?"

"Indeed," she answered, perturbed by his

clipped tone. "I've met you."

"Indeed." His abruptness was dismissive as he executed another series of turns just before the music ended, then led her from the dance floor to her aunt's side. "Thank you, Lady Jocelyn," he said barely above a whisper and, keeping his gaze locked on hers, bowed over her hand, giving it a light squeeze.

A delicious quiver ran down her spine, stunning her. He was handsome and she felt drawn to him, despite the intimidating countenance he displayed when observing her through his penetrating stare. Yet before she could reply, he'd disappeared in the crowd, and she little time to wonder at this as her next partner claimed her attention.

Even so, going through the steps of the cotillion, she considered if the Viscount could be Ellen's blackmailer.

When the orchestra took a break, Jossie found Lady Bolton at her elbow. "Come, Jossie, stroll with me on the veranda."

With a balmy breeze blowing through the trees, it was cooler outside, and a number of others shared the same idea, making private conversation difficult. Mindful of an audience, Beatrice linked her arm through Jossie's and leaned closer to half whisper, "I plan to tell George everything after the ball tonight."

Jossie heard the anxiety in her friend's voice. "Has something happened? You sound worried."

Beatrice glanced over her shoulder, then

pulled Jossie into the darker shadows of the house. "He's here."

"The blackmailer?" Jossie began to search among the couples on the terrace for Stangate's dark head and broad shoulders.

Beatrice's hold on her arm tightened. "Don't look about, or he'll guess that I've told you," she cautioned.

"Yes, but he already—"

"Ah, there you are, Cousin," Rupert drawled as he advanced on her with Sir Percy Carew in tow. "Sir Percy was saying how desirous he was to dance with you."

Jossie bit her lip to keep from uttering an unladylike retort. She'd like nothing better than to ring a peal over his head for hinting to Mr. Carlisle that they shared an understanding. Nor did she care for his unctuousness friend, Sir Percy. Instead, she checked her anger and managed a weak smile. "How thoughtful, Sir Percy, but my dance card is full."

Sir Percy looked from Jossie to Beatrice, forcing Jossie to make the introductions. "Lady Bolton," he said acknowledging her with a nod of his head before addressing Jossie. "I told Malton it would likely be so, Lady Jocelyn. Perhaps another time, then?"

"Yes," she said as the strains of a country reel started up. "You'll excuse us, please." She took Beatrice's arm and guided her past the two gentlemen, only to encounter Stangate as he stood to one side of the French doors, glaring at them. As they passed by the Viscount, Jossie felt her friend's shudder under her fingertips.

"I believe I'll find George and ask him to leave early," Beatrice said, without giving Stangate a glance. "Come for tea tomorrow, and we'll talk."

Jossie watched Beatrice make her way through the crowd, then turned back toward the door, but Stangate was no longer there. She was prevented from scanning the ballroom for him as her next partner engaged her.

~~~~~

All Beatrice could think about was leaving before he could meet with George and tell him of the affair. She was on her way to the card room where George said he'd be when she spotted her nemesis coming toward her. He stopped by a door and opened it.

"In here for a word, if you please."

Beatrice met his hard gaze and pulled her skirts tighter to her as she breezed past him through the door and into a small parlor. Though empty, it was lit by a candelabra. Making her way toward a couch with two matching armchairs, she stood before a black veined marble fireplace and faced him as he closed the door and slowly advanced to the other side of the fireplace.

"You've failed to deliver the goods."

"You're asking me to betray my country," she said, barely above a whisper.

"If you don't, your husband learns of your affair," he growled.

"Purely a lapse in judgment. Bolton will understand," she said with a tinkling laugh that sounded hallow even to her. Her stomach twisted in revolt as she prayed to maintain her false bravado.

"Your marriage—"

"Stop, enough," Beatrice stated emphatically, squaring her shoulders. "I intend to tell Bolton all of it. I cannot live this lie."

"You'll be branded a doxy. Polite society will shun you."

"Bolton will not denounce me publically."

"I, on the other hand, will let it become common knowledge." His smirk promised vengeance.

She shook her head. "It matters not, for I won't betray my country, and—and George will forgive me."

"Think again, my lady," he sneered. "I'll produce others who will describe your unusual birthmark to him."

His threat nearly brought her to her knees, for George would not forgive such damnable proof. However did this fiendish scoundrel come by such a personal detail? Still, she'd beg George's forgiveness, plead for his mercy on her knees if she had to. Through quivering lips, she said, "I cannot, will not do what you ask, but I will tell him you are a traitor to England."

"You rotten bitch," he growled and viciously slapped her.

The force of the blow caused her to lose her balance, and she staggered back toward the couch. With murder in his eyes, he grabbed a heavy angel candelabra off the mantel. Beatrice frantically scrambled around the couch, then turned for the door, praying she'd reach it in time to scream for help.

Chapter 8

Finally a moment to herself, Jossie left the ballroom for the repairing room on the first floor. During the last Scottish reel, the overheated room had her dabbing perspiration at her temple, dislodging a hairpin. Now making her way down the hall, she tucked a stray curl behind her ear, and stopped. A sound like a struggle, then a small cry came from behind a closed door just past the stairs. Cautiously, she stepped closer to it and listened, but heard only silence.

The voice had sounded like a woman's, so throwing caution to the wind, she opened the door and stuck her head in to catch sight of a dark figure going out a glass-paned door that led outside. The room was dimly lit by a branch of candles that stood on a small table and wildly flickered from the draft from the open door. Quickly, Jossie moved around the sofa and stepped through the door, looking all about, but she neither saw nor heard anyone. Turning back, she gasped at the sight of a woman lying on the floor behind the sofa.

Bending over the inert form, Jossie brought her hand up to her mouth as bile rose up in her throat, choking off a scream. Beatrice Bolton's unseeing honey brown eyes stared up at Jossie as a halo of blood pooled about her head. A bloody silver cherub candlestick lay on the floor next to her.

A noise jolted Jossie out of her shocked daze. She whirled about to see Stangate closing the door to the hallway behind him and advancing into the room.

"I saw you come in," he said, his expression unreadable as he stepped toward her. When Jossie looked down at Beatrice, he followed her gaze and, seeing the body, reached out and pulled her toward him in an embrace. Fear should have consumed her—after all, wasn't she alone with a blackmailer? Instead, his presence assuaged her overwrought nerves, giving her a sense that all would be well.

"Are you all right?" he asked, releasing her to take hold of her upper arms and search her face.

She nodded dumbly.

"Did you see anyone?"

She pointed at the opened side door. "A man."

"Did you get a good look at him?"

She shook her head.

"You're sure? You can't identify him?"

"No."

"Did you hear anything?"

"Yes, I was in the hall and heard a scuffle—and a woman's cry. It's why I entered." She turned her head to look down, but he placed his hand on the side of her face and forced her to focus on him.

"Don't look," he commanded. "Could you identify anything?" She frowned and he added, "Understand any words, or recognize a voice?"

"No." Somehow she found enough equanimity to ask, "Why are you here?"

His eyes narrowed but never left hers. "I saw you leave the ballroom and hoped to speak with you in a less noisy area."

"What—What's to be done?" She twisted to look at her friend, but he used his strength to keep her facing him. Her gaze caught the matching silver cherub candlestick on the far end of the mantle. Tears began to leak from her eyes.

His gaze cut to the figure on the floor before he drew out his linen handkerchief handed it to her. Tucking her under his arm, he drew her toward the door. "Dry your tears and go home."

"But I—"

"No argument," he growled, then said more gently, "you cannot be involved, say nothing of this to anyone. I'll handle everything."

Keeping her back to the room, he waited for her to gain her composure before reaching for the door handle. She placed her hand over his to stop him from opening the door. "Will you tell me what happens?"

Frowning, his piercing stare bore into her eyes, and he nodded. "I'll come by and take you for a drive tomorrow or the next day." He opened the door and glanced out into the hall, then put a hand to the small of her back and gave her a gentle push. "Now go, and say nothing of this to anyone."

She scurried down the hall to the ballroom where she found Lady Welbeck looking for her.

"There you are, Jossie. We've church in the morning, so I'm ready to leave as soon as I make my goodbyes to our hosts."

Numbly, Jossie fell in with these plans and went to order the coach before rejoining her aunt.

"Something is amiss," Aunt Cassie said conspiratorially. When Jossie gave her an inquiring look, she explained, "The Marchioness seemed distracted, upset even, and said Raynham was tied up with the Earl of Bolton, and that she'd relay our adieux."

Jossie's stomach plummeted as she realized Lord Bolton was, in all likelihood, learning about his wife's murder and could only imagine how such news would affect him. She also was thankful that Stangate had spirited her out of the parlor. Now, she was anxious to quit the Marquess's house, yet knowing she'd forever remember the horrid scene in the small parlor where Beatrice's lifeless body lay.

But on the ride home, another more sinister thought assailed her. What if Stangate was Beatrice's killer? Granted, the open door to the side yard had been the killer's means of escape. And he'd barely made it out the door before Jossie had stuck her head in the parlor.

Still, she didn't have any way of knowing from which direction Stangate had come. He might not have followed her from the ballroom as he'd claimed. Instead, he might have gone around to a rear door, then entered the small parlor to find her standing over poor Beatrice.

Another even more ominous thought came to mind. All of Stangate's questions were about whether or not she could identify Beatrice's killer and exactly what she'd seen and heard. He hadn't asked her what her reason was for being in the parlor. She had volunteered that.

Then again, who else but the blackmailer had reason to kill Beatrice? Might Stangate think Jossie suspected he was the killer?

An apprehensive shudder skidded down her spine. Had she let the horror of Beatrice's death overshadow her good sense to the point that she had willingly accepted solace in the arms of the very person who killed Beatrice?

Heaven help her! Could she be his next victim?

~~~~~

It was a long time before Jossie sought her bed after the Raynham's ball. She was overcome with grief and, sitting in the chair before a small fire in her bedchamber, mourned Beatrice's demise with copious tears. While she had only known the older lady for a few short weeks, it was hard to contemplate how someone could brutally bludgeon such a beautiful woman. She cried for Lord Bolton, knowing how devastated he must be over losing his beautiful, vibrant wife.

With the nearing of dawn, when she finally laid her head on the pillow, she kept seeing Beatrice's unseeing eyes, surrounded by a pool of blood. Neither could Jossie forget her initial reaction when Stangate appeared at the parlor's door. Knowing he'd been blackmailing Beatrice, she should have been weary. Instead, she'd derived a sense of comfort and protection from him. How could her senses delude her so?

But it wasn't Beatrice's blank stare that filled her dreams. No, it was a pair of piercing blue eyes that bored into hers as he swept her around a ballroom one minute and, in the next, chased her through dark, eerie halls.

After a short, restless sleep, she rose early, tired and melancholy. She let Becky fuss over her toilette for church, as she nibbled on a scone and sipped a cup of hot chocolate. She was choosing a pair of earbobs when a knock on her door heralded Dilhorne with the Viscount's calling card. "I took the liberty of placing him in the drawing room, my lady."

Good heavens, she'd hadn't expected to see him before noon, believing he'd be tied up with the magistrate into the early morning hours. Besides that, should she even meet with him, since he was the prime suspect for Beatrice's murder?

"Is everything all right, miss?" Becky asked.

Noticing the maid's worried expression, Jossie marshaled her nerve to meet the Viscount. He certainly wouldn't harm her in her aunt's home with the servants all about.

Moments later, Jossie entered the drawing room to encounter Stangate with one arm draped across the mantle, staring down at the orange and red flames of a coal fire. He looked up and revealed dark circles under his solemn eyes, attesting to the fact he'd yet to seek his bed that night, though he had changed his evening attire to an olive superfine jacket, cream breeches, and a pristine cravat with a black pearl stickpin. His appearance certainly wasn't that of a cold-blooded murderer.

He stepped toward her. "How are you fairing this morning?"

"I believe better than you, my lord," she replied gesturing from him to take a seat on the blue damask settee. "It appears you've yet to seek out your bed?"

He waited for her to sit in an armchair facing him before taking his seat. "I've spent the time with the magistrate and Lord Bolton."

"How is Lord Bolton?" she asked fighting back tears of sympathy for Beatrice's husband.

"Devastated, as to be expected, and angry," he answered matter-of-factly. He went on to explain how events unfolded after she'd left the ball. "Raynham sent for the magistrate, Sir John Fielding, a no nonsense man who took charge, questioning servants and several guests who still remained." He gave her a knowing look. "Sir John wants to talk with you also?"

"Of—of course," she stammered, daunted by the very thought.

"You must testify as to what you saw."

"I didn't really see anything," she protested, wondering if he believed her.

"Perhaps not, but it's the magistrate's job to interrogate anyone who may have seen or heard anything that might be connected to Lady Bolton's murder." His piercing blue eyes bore into hers. "You didn't see or hear anything, correct?"

There it was again, his questioning what she'd witnessed.

For an answer, she shook her head, and he leaned back in the chair. "Then you've nothing to worry about. Furthermore, I'll bring Sir John here and will remain with you throughout the interview."

She didn't quite know how to take that. Should she be concerned over his interest in the investigation? Recalling how much comfort his presence had brought her last night, she was far from feeling that now. Hindsight forced her to question his involvement with Beatrice and his timely appearance in the parlor.

"Does Lady Welbeck know what happened?"

His question startled her. "Good heavens, whatever shall I tell my aunt?"

"I suggest you tell her—"

"Lord Stangate, pardon my delay." Lady Welbeck swept into the drawing room as the Viscount rose to his feet. "My abigail just told me you were here." She turned to Jossie. "What, no tea cart, my dear?"

With a raised eyebrow, Stangate gave Jossie a pointed look. "May I?"

Despite her mistrust of him, she heaved a sigh of relief. Really, she was a coward at heart. "Please do so, for I've no idea where to begin."

"What's this?" Lady Welbeck asked, taking in the two of them.

Stangate waited until her aunt sat in a chair next to Jossie before resuming his seat. Then he proceeded to describe how Jossie came upon Lady Bolton's body and his role in directing her to leave the Raynhams' immediately.

Aunt Cassie turned to Jossie and exclaimed, "Good heavens, Jossie, why didn't you tell me?"

"I instructed her not to say anything until I had a chance to speak with the magistrate," Stangate said. He glanced over at Jossie and added, "Lady Jocelyn will be required to testify before the magistrate about how she discovered Lady Bolton."

Her aunt frowned. "Yes, I can understand that. But what a nasty business."

"You need not concern yourself, my lady," he said. "I was just explaining to Lady Jocelyn that I will bring Sir John Fielding here tomorrow, and lend her my support."

"Thank you, Stangate," Lady Welbeck replied feelingly. "Your assistance is most appreciated. I fear I'd be of little help to her."

A time was set for Stangate and the magistrate to meet in Mount Street on the next day. No sooner had the door closed behind the Viscount than her aunt turned on Jossie and demanded, "Now, young lady, I think it's past time you tell me *everything* that has been going on."

Chapter 9

Once Lady Welbeck had learned the entire story, between vexation and utter horror, she'd not minced words about Jossie's inexcusable behavior. First, she'd poked her nose in a room uninvited—and without knocking, then was alone in a parlor with the Viscount with the door closed—well, not exactly alone since Beatrice's body was on the floor. And then, Jossie had failed to notify her aunt immediately of her involvement in the murder.

Of course, it was not the *entire* story. Jossie felt she had to protect Lady Bolton's reputation, so she judiciously left out the fact that Beatrice was being blackmailed for her affair with Stangate.

Also, she excluded how she'd dressed like a youth and broke into the Viscount's study to steal love letters—and gotten caught by Stangate.

And she omitted Mary Ellen-er, Eleanor Addison's charade, for which Ellen was now being blackmailed.

Along with Jossie's suspicion that Stangate was the blackmailer, which made him the prime suspect for Beatrice's murder.

"Really, Jossie, I cannot believe you didn't tell me," Lady Welbeck admonished her. "And never say it slipped your mind."

"I could never say that, Aunt Cassie, for it was quite dreadful and the last thing I wanted to dwell on."

"No, I'm sure you didn't. At least Stangate will be on hand for the horrible business of you being interrogated by the magistrate."

The ladies proceeded to St. George's Church for Sunday serve, and afterwards spent a quiet and uneventful day at home. Aunt Cassie even instructed Dilhorne that they were not at home to afternoon callers.

But promptly at eleven on Monday morning, Jossie sat under Lady Welbeck's critical eye when Dilhorne admitted Viscount Stangate and Sir John Fielding to the drawing room.

Introductions were made, a tea tray called for, then everyone found a seat before Sir John pulled out a notebook and pencil from his breast pocket and gave Jossie a fatherly smile. "Now, Lady Jocelyn, what do you remember about the events of Saturday night?"

Sir John was a stout man in his mid-fifties with white hair worn unfashionably long. While he rested benevolent brown eyes on Jossie, she doubted his gaze missed anything. She licked her lower lip, steeled her already straight spine, and explained how on her way to the retiring room, she'd heard what sounded like a scuffle, then a woman's cry before all was silent.

Thinking someone might be in trouble, she'd opened the door to see a man going out the door to the side yard and went to it to peer out, but saw no one. Turning back into the room, she found Lady Bolton on the floor with the sliver candlestick holder lying next to her.

"You didn't see anyone else?" Sir John asked.

"No."

"When did Lord Stangate come upon the scene?"

"Almost immediately," she said, cutting her eyes toward the Viscount. "He—he ushered me out of the room, explaining that I must not be found there."

"Very considerate of him." Sir John's gaze settled on Stangate for several long moments. "And you, Stangate, what brought you to that parlor?"

"I saw Lady Jocelyn leave the ballroom and desired a private word with her," he said unruffled.

Sir John's bushy white eyebrows rose. "A private word, you say? What might that be about?"

Stangate turned his gaze on Jossie, who flushed under his warm regard. "I'd intended to ask Lady Jocelyn to drive out with me the next day."

Even as Jossie blushed under such scrutiny, her mind reeled over how easily Stangate could voice such a lie. If he'd wanted to ask her to drive out with him, there'd been opportunities in the ballroom or while they'd waltzed.

Furthermore, he'd shown little interest previously toward her when they met socially. There was the kiss he'd bestowed upon her at the brothel, but that had been nothing more than a ploy to hide her identity from Mrs. Dunlap. And while it curled her toes, he seemed unaffected by it and had never tried to kiss her again.

Fortunately for Jossie's nerves, the interview concluded soon after, and Sir John left. Lady Welbeck, however, invited Stangate to stay for nuncheon, then began to pelt him with questions about what transpired at the Raynhams after she and Jossie left the ball.

In the middle of professing nothing of import occurred, Dilhorne announced, "The Honorable Rupert Malton, my lady."

Rupert strode in and drew up short when he spotted Stangate standing by the fireplace. After greeting the ladies, he addressed the Viscount. "Surprised to see you here, my lord?" When Stangate acknowledged Rupert with a mere nod, he turned back to Jossie. "I'd have come sooner, but I only just heard about you witnessing Lady Bolton's murder."

Jossie narrowed her eyes on him. "Who told you that?"

He took the chair the magistrate had so recently vacated. "I paid my respects to Lord Bolton, and he told me you were there."

"It was not exactly like that," Jossie said.

"Still, if the murderer knows you saw him, he'll likely come after you next." His walnut eyes held a look of concern. "You're not safe living here with just Lady Welbeck, Jossie. You need to return to Manchester Square where I can protect you."

"You're mistaken, Malton," Stangate interjected, coming to stand next to where Jossie sat. "She didn't witness the murder, nor see the murderer. She heard something, which we assume was the murderer escaping through a side door. When she entered the room, it was empty."

Listening to Stangate, Jossie wondered why he stressed that she'd not seen or heard anything. Add to that, while they stood next to Beatrice's body, he'd pressured her to reveal all that she knew and saw. The more she considered the matter, the greater her suspicion was that he'd killed poor Beatrice.

Which left her with a hallow feeling in her chest.

But at least Rupert accepted the Viscount's word and didn't say anything more about her returning home. Still, it became apparent that her cousin intended to stay until Stangate left, forcing Aunt Cassie to extend an invitation for him to join them for nuncheon.

Thankfully, Dilhorne, having been with Lady Welbeck for eons, recognized her ladyship's silent disapproval of Jossie's cousin when told to set a fourth place at the table and sonorously suggested, "Perhaps my lady would find it more comfortable to partake it in here?"

A short time later, Dilhorne reappeared with a delectable tea. Unfortunately, even though the atmosphere was less formal, conversation remained stilted. Soon after, the guests went about their respective ways, and both ladies breathed a sigh of relief.

"Imagine Rupert mooching a meal off me, Jossie," Lady Welbeck groused. "He really is a most disagreeable fellow."

"Indeed, Aunt Cassie."

"Yes, besides that, it's plain as pikestaff those two have no liking for the other. With any luck, we'll have seen the last of them."

Later that afternoon, Adrian entered White's in Saint James's Street and encountered the Earl of Bolton, who'd sent a note requesting Adrian share a brandy with him. Taking a seat at a table tucked in a corner, Bolton signaled to a footman to bring a bottle and goblets.

"Have you spoken with Sir John recently?" Bolton asked.

"Matter of fact, I saw him this morning at Lady Welbeck's as he interviewed Lady Jocelyn." Bolton's aristocratic features appeared more gaunt than lean with a heaviness about his eyes that suggested lack of sleep, all of which spoke to the Earl's grieving for his wife.

The footman arrived with brandy and glasses, and as Bolton poured them each a drink, he asked, "Then you don't know?"

"I've heard of no new developments," he said, accepting a glass.

Bolton's eyes burned with anger. "Sir John considers me a possible suspect in Beatrice's death."

Adrian lazily lowered his eyelids, though his senses went on high alert. "Did he say why?"

Bolton shook his head. "He's threatened to search my home."

"Any idea what he's looking for?"

"No, so I started looking through Beatrice's things." He stopped and his eyes hardened. "I found a sort of journal that she kept intermittently." He leaned closer to Adrian and with steel in his voice said, "Your name is prominent in the last several entries."

Adrian eased back in his chair and took another sip of brandy, contemplating how much to tell the Earl, and decided to make a clean breast of the affair. "I met Lady Bolton at a masquerade, but she gave her name as Beatrice Winslow."

"That's her maiden name," Bolton supplied. His narrowed gaze never left Adrian's.

"I didn't know she was your wife." *Hell*, he thought, *she led me to believe she was widowed.* "The first I knew she was married to you was when I encountered the two of you together at the Kedleston's ball. I'm sorry, Bolton."

For several minutes, the Earl silently stared at Adrian with his jaw clenching and unclenching. Finally, he leaned back in his chair and released a breath. "Thank you for accepting the blame, but her written words admitted to perusing you. She was angry with me," he said dolefully. "She'd learned I had a mistress and meant to punish me.

What she didn't know was I'd given Nicole her congé six months ago." He dropped his eyes to his glass. "I loved my wife."

There was no suitable reply to this, so Adrian remained silent and sipped his drink. He didn't see any need to bring up Beatrice's billet-doux and fervently hoped she'd destroyed them.

Bolton leaned back in his chair. "I have no idea who killed Beatrice or why. But I didn't," he declared emphatically. "Stangate, I'd like you to help me find out who did."

"Why me?" *I diddled your wife, so why ask me?* Adrian wondered.

"You've a reputation at the Home Office for getting things done," Bolton replied.

"Did you consider that I might be the murderer?"

Bolton nodded. "I did, but while you're reputed to be ruthless in your pursuits, your integrity has never been questioned." He shrugged a shoulder. "Besides, what would you gain by killing Beatrice?"

"You work for the Home Office. Have you enemies?"

Bolton sat with his lips pressed together for several moments deep in thought before he shook his head. "None who'd have reason to murder my wife."

"Did you notice anything different about Lady Bolton recently? Maybe her actions or the people she saw?"

Bolton also considered this before answering. "She seemed distracted, caught her woolgathering more often. She did met a young woman whom she'd apparently taken under her wing."

"Who is the woman?"

"Lady Jocelyn Graydon."

Why wasn't this a surprise? The minx was truly a magnet for trouble.

Bolton leaned closer to Adrian and crossed his arms on the table. "Help me find my wife's killer, Stangate?"

Adrian studied the Earl's haggard countenance before he drank the remainder of his drink and rose. "You've my word, I'll do my level best."

~~~~~

On Wednesday, Jossie received a morning visit from Ellen, who entered the drawing room with hands clasped in a pleading gesture.

"I need your help, Jossie. I know this is unexpected, but another note came," Ellen announced with a sob. "A street urchin delivered it to the house in Kensington just an hour ago."

"Come, sit down, Ellen," Jossie said, leading the distraught girl to the settee and sitting down beside her. "What did the note say?"

Untying the string of her reticule, Ellen produced a small folded missive and passed it to Jossie. "You may read it yourself, but he states I am to meet him tomorrow night at Vauxhall Gardens in the Rotunda when the fireworks go off."

"Good heavens, we've got to make plans," Jossie said, trying to hide her excitement. Here was a chance to discover the blackmailer's identity, and possibly Beatrice's killer. "You'll put him off, just as we discussed."

"Put off paying him," Ellen cried incredulously. "There's no way I can come close to gathering the funds he wants, even if I pawned every last trinket I have." A thought seemed to strike her, for her eyes grew wide, and she said in hushed tones, "What if he killed Beatrice? What if he tries to kill me?" Her voice rose to a squeak.

"First, do not admit you'll never have all the money," Jossie said, thinking furiously. "He won't kill you if he believes there's a chance you'll eventually pay him. We'll stick to our plan. I'll be there ahead of you, hiding in the Rotunda."

A frown wrinkled Ellen's brow. "But you can't prevent him from injuring me, or you if you're discovered."

"I'll carry a weapon."

Ellen's hand clutched Jossie's arm. "A weapon? What sort of weapon?"

Jossie hadn't thought ahead that far. "I'm not sure, but you *can* be sure I'll know how to use it to protect you. Now, tomorrow night, you and Miss Trundle will come collect me, and we'll all go to Vauxhall Gardens together. If nothing else, I can follow the despicable cur and find out where he lives, and then who he is." She leaned back into the settee. "Leave everything to me, Ellen. All will come about."

Chapter 10

Over tea that afternoon, Jossie approached Lady Welbeck with her plan to make up a party the next night for Vauxhall Gardens to meet several of Ellen's friends. This small prevarication proved enough discouragement for her aunt to bow out attending an outing of young people.

"Since Miss Trundle will chaperone Miss Whiddon, there's no need for me to go," her aunt said, considering the matter. "No need for a hackney, either, Jossie. Take my carriage instead," Aunt Cassie instructed. "I'll not be going out as I acquired Miss Austen's *Sense and Sensibility* from the lending library yesterday and would much prefer a quiet night at home reading for a change."

Mentally, Jossie smiled to herself. Things were going according to plan. She sent a note to Kensington, informing Ellen that they had the use of her aunt's carriage for their foray to Vauxhall and asked Dilhorne to reserve a supper box for the three of them. After some thought, she decided the best choice of a weapon would be a knife. Aunt Cassie did kept a small pistol in her bed stand, and while a gun might be preferable, it would be easier to pilfer a knife from the kitchen.

So, upon returning from a dinner and card party of one of her aunt's cronies, Jossie made a late night detour to the kitchen. There, she borrowed a sharp paring knife, and after sheathing it in a small hand towel, tucked it into her evening reticule.

The following day dawned bright with nary a cloud in the sky. By evening a light breeze sprung up, and with the moon shining brightly and few clouds about, the night promised to remain pleasant. Shortly before eight, Lady Welbeck's crested carriage pulled into the Coach Gate entrance of the pleasure gardens off Kennington Lane, and the ladies disembarked to stroll the walkways, taking in the various statues, stone arches, covered arbors, and the Rotunda before locating their supper box across from the Orchestra Building.

Ordinarily, the girls would have enjoyed listening to the quartet playing atop the building and watching London's diverse citizenry dancing or promenading along the Grand Walk. But both felt apprehensive for the upcoming encounter with the blackmailer. In particular, Ellen seemed incapable of dissembling in front of Miss Trundle, her conversation distracted, thus leaving it to Jossie to entertain their chaperone.

At one point, Miss Trundle's attention was

diverted when an old acquaintance stopped by their supper box. As the two elderly ladies greeted each other, Ellen leaned closer to Jossie and whispered, "Did you bring a weapon?"

Jossie nodded, but was reluctant to tell Ellen it was only a small knife tucked in her reticule. Granted, the knife's slim blade looked quite lethal, but how she would go about wielding it, Jossie wasn't quite sure. In fact, she'd spent most of the day preoccupied visualizing gruesome scenarios to disarm the blackmailer as he accosted Ellen, like imagining drawing the knife across the blackmailer's hand that held a gun on her petrified friend.

Or plunging the blade in his upraised arm before he could strike a hysterically sobbing Ellen with his fist.

Or just like the knife thrower hitting the bull's eye at Astley's Circus, throwing the blade at the blackmailer's heart seconds before he used his own to slit Ellen's throat.

She even pondered over how close she needed to be to stab the scoundrel while staying beyond his reach. Or was that even possible?

"What is it?" Ellen asked when Jossie wasn't more forthcoming.

"A knife," she whispered.

Ellen looked nonplussed. "Do—do you think that is sufficient protection?"

"I promise not to let anything happen to you." Jossie meant it too. She'd do everything within her power to see that no harm came to Ellen.

No more was said, for Miss Trundle made the girls known to her friend, Mrs. Nye. When the matronly widow revealed she'd come with her sister and her sister's husband and friends, Jossie insisted Mrs. Nye join their party, hoping the other woman's presence would keep Miss Trundle occupied while she and Ellen kept the rendezvous with the blackmailer.

Half past eight, just before dusk, they ordered arrack punch and dined on an assortment of cold meats, including wafer thin slices of ham, salad, cheese. Jossie hardly did justice to the meal, though the lemon tarts had tempted her.

Fortunately, though the air had cooled, the night remained clear. Twenty minutes before the fireworks display, Jossie and Ellen persuaded Miss Trundle that the multitude of colored lamps hanging in the trees and arbors brightly lit most of the pathways and arbors, making it safe for the two of them to stroll along the gravel paths.

Permission granted, the girls set out arm in arm, ignoring the many statues and temples set in among the tall yew hedges and stately trees as they made their way toward the Rotunda, a large, circular, temple-like structure with a pointed dome ceiling. They were careful to avoid the darker walkways, where one might be accosted by pickpockets or encounter prostitutes plying their trade.

Ten minutes before the planned fireworks, Jossie bade Ellen to lag behind while she quickly made her way along the path to the Rotunda. As she neared the building, Jossie noticed that most of the lanterns were uncharacteristically extinguished leaving the pathway in an ominous gloom.

Cautiously, she entered the structure, where a few lamps remained lit, putting the open floor with its numerous pillars and recesses in eerie darkness. A moment of fear shattered her resolve, and she sent a silent prayer heavenward that the blackmailer wasn't already there, hiding and watching her.

She'd purposely worn a black cloak with a hood, rendering her nearly invisible as she tiptoed around the curved perimeter, keeping close to the dark shadowy walls. She chose one of the numerous, shallow-arched alcoves that gave her a perspective of the entrance and flattened herself against the wall. Reaching inside her reticule, she slid the knife out and gripped it tightly by her side as she waited for Ellen and the blackmailer.

Minutes passed. The dark shadows seemed to possess lives of their own, as Jossie's eyes peered about the gloomy rotunda. Fireworks went off, but no one entered the building, and she began to wonder if she'd picked the wrong structure. Still maintaining a tight clasp on the knife, she pulled her mantle closely around her and started toward the entrance when a dark figure emerged from another alcove. Stifling a scream, she jerked back, defensively bringing both her arms up, the knife reflecting what little light there was, and pivoted on her foot. Before she ran a half dozen steps, two large hands vice gripped her upper arms, preventing her escape.

"What are you doing here?"

Stangate's growl was like a slap to her face. With her heart in her throat, and she fired back, "W—what are you doing here?"

"Bloody hell! You've got more hair than wit." His growl was little above a whisper, his anger palpable. He released one arm and reached out to take the knife from her clenched fist and tucked it inside the pocket of his jacket. "Come, I'll take you back to your party." He firmly held her elbow and started for the entrance with her in tow.

"How do you know whom I'm with?" She was almost running to keep up with his long strides. "And who are you with, my lord?"

Rather than answer, he asked, "Where is Miss Whiddon and her chaperone?"

Her mind was ripe with her own questions. Where was Ellen? Why hadn't she come? And most importantly, what was Stangate doing, hiding in the Rotunda? Screwing up her courage, she asked, "Are you here to meet someone, my lord?"

"You should know better than to roam about the gardens by yourself, Jossie" he admonished.

"I-I got separated from Miss Whiddon." She was nearly breathless trying to keep up with his long strides and angry that she felt the need to justify herself. Besides, he was ignoring her questions.

They came upon the back side of the Orchestra Building, and she dug in her heels, bring them to a halt. "I prefer to go the rest of the way by myself."

His cold stare and stolid expression were designed to make her quake in her leather half boots. But she didn't believe he would knowing hurt her, and really, what could happen to her in a public garden with people mulling about, preparing to leave now that the fireworks had ceased?

"Allow me the pleasure of accompanying you, Lady Jocelyn." His voice was a mocking purr.

He took her hand and threaded it through his elbow and began to stroll more leisurely down the Grand Walk toward the supper box. As they neared, Jossie saw Ellen and Miss Trundle standing in front of it waiting for her.

Stangate deposited her next to Miss Trundle and bowed over her hand. "Will you drive out with me tomorrow afternoon, Lady Jocelyn?"

He may have asked, but his tone and the severity of his expression suggested she'd little choice. Reluctantly, she accepted with as much aplomb as she could muster and bade him good night. As he turned aside, she watched to see where he went, but soon lost him in the crowd.

"Oh, Jossie, where were you?" Ellen cried as Jossie turned to go into the supper box. "I've been so worried."

Plopping down on a chair before her legs gave out from under her, Jossie took a deep breath to calm her racing heart. "Ellen, what happened to you?"

The young woman cast a cautious eye toward her chaperone before she said, "I was behind you walking toward the Rotunda when a man wearing a dark cloak and wide-brimmed hat stepped out from behind a statue and . . . and asked for directions to the fireworks area. That's how I lost sight of you."

Understanding Ellen could divulge little else in Miss Trundle's presence, Jossie let the matter drop as they gathered their things to leave. On the walk to the Coach Gate where Lady Welbeck's carriage awaited them, Jossie and Ellen strolled slightly ahead of Miss Trundle, allowing Ellen to tell Jossie about the man who'd accosted her.

Because lamps had been extinguished, Ellen had been unable to see his face deeply shadowed by the wide brim of his hat. He did agree to give her another week to acquire the funds, however. "But after that," Ellen whispered, her head bent toward Jossie, "he said he'd find Harry and tell him all. Jossie, he said he had irrefutable proof that I'm not Mary Ellen Whiddon. What am I going to do?"

"Did he say what proof he had?" Jossie asked.

"No, and I don't know what he could have other than an obituary for Mary Ellen."

Jossie considered this before adding, "He could have statements from neighbors that Mary Ellen had perished in the epidemic, or a statement from the clergyman who buried her." As they waited for the Welbeck carriage to pull up to the gate, she said, "Let me think about this, Ellen. There must be something we can do."

As Miss Trundle entered the carriage, Ellen whispered, "How did you come upon Lord Stangate?"

"I stumbled into him returning to the supper box," Jossie hedged. It wasn't exactly a lie. She was simply omitting that the Viscount had been hiding in the Rotunda, which posed other, more sinister questions. If Stangate was in the Rotunda, then who confronted Ellen? Was Stangate in cahoots with that man? Or was there an altogether different explanation for Stangate being in the Rotunda tonight?

Jossie's heart sorely hoped that was so.

~~~~~

At home in his study later that night, Adrian poured a generous amount of brandy into a goblet before sitting in a wingback before a coal fire. Leaning his head back against the burgundy leather, he considered what his informant had relayed yesterday to him about Carew meeting with a French émigré at a tavern in Cheapside. The informant claimed to overhear Carew say he'd planned an assignation with someone tonight in the Rotunda at Vauxhall Gardens around ten of the clock.

Deciding it could be a credible lead, Adrian had half a dozen men watching the perimeter of the Rotunda. With so many unlit lamps around the surrounding area, he cautiously made his way into the darkened interior and hid. If luck favored them, they'd catch Carew and a fellow co-conspirator.

Instead, just before the fireworks started, a

woman in a black cloak entered and tucked herself in an archway mere feet from his own hiding place. Then after several minutes, she emerged from the shadows with a knife in one hand and started for the entrance. He'd revealed himself, intending to find out who she was and get some answers.

The moment she'd bumped into him, her lavender scent assailed his senses, leaving no doubt it was Jossie. Despite his anger at finding her there, he was consumed with an unquenchable desire to pull her into his arms and kiss the infuriating minx senseless.

His lips twitched as memories of their first meeting in the brothel came to mind. The vixen had captivated his interest from the first moment he stared into her large luminous, almost sliver eyes framed by rich dark brown hair curling about her svelte form. She had plenty of spunk, too, he thought, and a laugh escaped him as he remembered their encounter in this study.

Problem was she bewitched him in other ways as well. He took a long pull of the brandy. He still recalled the surging desire that overtook him when he'd kissed her at the brothel, and since then, she'd plagued his thoughts day and night. In fact, he found himself going to the vary balls and breakfasts he'd always shied away from seeking her.

He frowned. Suppose she wasn't the innocent debutant. Was it possible she'd been at the Rotunda for a lover's tryst? If so, why was she clutching a knife?

He shook his head and rose up to grab the bell pull for Paddison. Barely a minute passed when Adrian's tall, lean butler entered. He possessed a head of iron grey hair, a long face and a Roman nose, and a rigid bearing that proclaimed his background as an army sergeant, who often assisted Adrian with assignments.

"Paddison, I've a chore for you," Adrian began. "Set a watch on the back gate of Lady Welbeck's townhouse. Tell them to follow Lady Jocelyn and make note where she goes and who she meets. And Paddison." Adrian paused to give his butler a knowing look. "Most likely the lady will be slipping the leash after dark dressed as a lad."

"Very good, my lord." He reached for Adrian's glass. "May I refresh your drink?"

Accepting the refilled tumbler, Adrian took a thoughtful sip. What was he missing? Things didn't add up, but he intended to get answers—starting tomorrow with the delectable and somewhat danger-prone Lady Jocelyn.

Chapter 11

A fretful night's sleep convinced Jossie what her next move should be. Now, mid-morning she sat in the drawing room with Eliza Parson's Gothic tale, *The Castle of Wolfenbach*, opened on her lap and stared uncomprehendingly at the printed words. Mentally she reviewed the events of last night, and one thing was apparent. Stangate's appearance in the Rotunda at the exact time the blackmailer was to meet Ellen was beyond suspicious.

She knew from past experience, if he were Ellen's blackmailer, then the likely place he'd keep the evidence to unmask her friend's true identity was his desk.

Which gave credence to her next course of action—breaking into Stangate's townhouse again. As she contemplated what needed to be done, Dilhorne entered.

"Excuse me, Lady Jocelyn, Lord Stangate is here to see you."

"Stangate?" What was he doing here? It

was as though her thoughts had conjured him up.

He bowed his balding head. "Shall I show him in?"

"Thank you, Dilhorne." She placed the book on a small side table and rose to shake out the creases in her skirt while waiting for the Viscount.

Moments later, Stangate's tall frame and wide shoulders nearly filled the doorway as he entered looking grim. His eyes roamed her from head to toe.

It struck her that she might be entertaining the devil, or at the very least Beatrice's murderer. She drew a deep breath, imagining herself as a Roman gladiator facing a lion—

No, more like a a panther—to match his dark coloring and preference for black togs—a predatory big cat that pounced and devoured its prey. Even his blue eyes, which could freeze one's blood with his piercing stare, had the look of a hunter.

After exchanging greetings, she sat on the settee and gestured for him to sit across from her. "What may I do for you at such an early hour, my lord?"

"I came to return this." He reached inside his black superfine jacket and unsheathed the kitchen knife he'd taken from her last night. Then, holding onto the tip of the blade, he formally laid it over his other forearm and bent over, offering it to her. He stood poised thusly until Jossie gathered her wits about her and grasped the knife's handle.

"Er, thank you, my lord."

As he straightened his back, he said, "I also want an explanation for why you were at Vauxhall Gardens last night, hiding in the Rotunda, brandishing that knife."

Well, that was the last thing she wanted to discuss. "Tea, my lord?"

His gaze hardened. "Cut line, Jossie. I want the truth."

So did she. Preparing to do battle, she squared her shoulders. "Why were you there, my lord?"

"Doing it much too brown, my dear. I'll have answers."

Well, he wasn't getting them. "Tell me, Stangate, why did you lie to my cousin, saying I never saw the murderer?"

"Malton was looking for an excuse to move you back to Manchester Square. Then, if he brandied it about that you saw the murderer escaping, that might make you his next target."

His reasoning was sound, yet it was disconcerting how quickly he appeared after Beatrice was murdered. And he still offered no explanation for hiding in the Rotunda last night.

Flipping up his coattails of his jacket, he took the seat next to her on the settee and demanded, "Please be good enough to explain your presence at Vauxhall last night?"

To keep from squirming under his unyielding glare, Jossie straightened her spine. "Unfortunately, my lord, I am not at liberty to say." She didn't think it possible for him to look any more menacing, but his face seemed to harden and his eyes narrowed on hers.

"Were you there to meet someone?"

So low did he speak, she had to strain to catch the words. Then, as his meaning struck her, she stood up and faced him as he followed suit. "I was not there for a tryst," she enunciated angrily before pointing to the door and continued. "I find you insulting. Please leave."

His glare softened along with his voice. "If you're in trouble, let me help you."

She shook her head. "I do not need nor want your help, my lord."

"It's Adrian."

She took a short, steading breath and shook her head.

"Then Stangate." He waited a moment, but when she didn't reply, he said, "This is far from over, Jossie. Though I don't know what you're about, it's a dangerous game you're playing. You'd do well to reconsider my help."

As he made to leave, she asked, "Does this visit mean we will not be driving out this afternoon?"

"It does." His lips curled in a wry smile. "Unfortunately, something has come up that demands my attention." With that, he gave her a short bow and left.

Moments later, Aunt Cassie entered the drawing room. "Was that Stangate who just left?" When Jossie acknowledged it was, she asked, "Did he bring any news about poor Lady Bolton?"

Thinking quickly, she pulled a small scrap

of linen out of the cuff of her sleeve. "Actually, he was at Vauxhall last night and was returning a handkerchief I'd left behind that he found."

"How . . . thoughtful of him." Her aunt frowned slightly as she sat in the chair beside Jossie. "My dear, I'm sure you know what you're doing, but truly, do you think you should encourage Stangate's attention?"

Jossie laughed. "His efforts to secure my attention, Aunt Cassie, are nothing more than a paltry effort to make himself more palatable to the *ton*."

"How can you say such a thing?"

"The man—"

"Gentleman, my dear, he is a nobleman."

Jossie nodded. "The gentleman is playing with the *ton*. After all, his reputation is at best that of a libertine."

"True, but people will talk, especially as Stangate is not known to participate in the Season, at least not in the regular way."

"You've no cause to worry, Aunt Cassie, for I've no intention of setting my cap at the Viscount."

Chapter 12

Before leaving Grosvenor Square for Mount Street that morning, Adrian had received a note from Lord Bolton requesting Adrian join the Earl for a late dinner at White's. When Adrian arrived at the club, he noted that few tables were occupied as most members where either already in the gaming rooms or still at home. Thus, he easily located Bolton sitting at his usual table tucked in a corner of the room, sipping a glass of brandy.

"Thank you for showing on such short notice," Bolton greeted him, his expression wan and grave as he poured a glass for Adrian. "I know it's only been a couple of days, but I'm hoping you have some news for me?"

Adrian shook his head. "None, though I've been making the rounds to various parties and balls, trying to catch a whiff of a lead." He gave the Earl a sympathetic look. "There's plenty of speculation about Lady Bolton's death, but I've heard nothing that we weren't already aware of or anything to suggest a possible motive."

Bolton reached inside his coat pocket and withdrew a missive, handing it to Adrian. "I went through the pockets of Beatrice's cloaks and gowns. Yesterday, I found that in a reticule."

Adrian unfolded the single sheet of foolscap with a faint watermark and read the blunt lettering scratched on the Grillon's stationary. "*If you don't want your husband to know of your affair, make copies of the documents he brings home from the Home Office. I'll tell you where to deliver them in one week. Say nothing unless you want all disclosed.*"

Adrian studied the note for several minutes. Here was not only a clue to Lady Bolton's murderer, but also a possible lead to the traitor who'd attacked the Home Office's administrative aides. Bolton worked with the Undersecretary at the Home Office, and Adrian suspected the documents allured to contained highly sensitive material. It appeared the perpetrator wanted information to sell.

He laid the missive on the table and, meeting Bolton's gaze, said tonelessly, "Someone was blackmailing Beatrice."

"So it appears."

Adrian eased back in his chair and thoughtfully drank his brandy. "Has anything recently gone missing? Noticed anything moved or out of place?"

"No." Bolton leaned closer and lowered his voice. "I kept the papers I brought home in the bottom draw of my desk which I had fortified along with a heavy lock installed. You'd have to splinter the desk to get the drawer out. Someone would have heard."

Out of habit, Adrian let his gaze lazily roam the room, which had filled with young bloods fortifying themselves before striking out for the gaming dens, and caught the eye of Rupert Malton. He saluted Adrian with a raised glass of wine from across the room where he sat sharing a bottle of claret with Sir Percy Carew. Adrian nodded in recognition before turning back to Bolton. "Have you told Sir John about this?"

Bolton shook his head. "The information is too sensitive, too damaging to Beatrice's reputation."

"I agree," he said, then gestured toward the note. "May I keep this?" At Bolton's nod, he picked it up and tucked it inside his jacket pocket. "At least we have a possible motive."

He spent the remainder of the dinner asking Bolton about his friends and acquaintances, and those who'd been to the Earl's home in recent weeks. Nothing out of the ordinary stood out. Thus, it was with misgivings that, while biding Bolton good night, he encouraged Bolton to take heart. "Something is bound to turn up."

The hour was advanced when he stepped out into Saint James Street and saluted an acquaintance entering the club, tapping his Malacca cane to his beaver top hat before starting toward Piccadilly. Streetlamps and carriages with their lanterns lit rolling past on the cobblestone streets provided enough light for Adrian to see his way to

Berkeley Street where he took a right.

Suddenly, two large men wearing dark clothes and caps pulled low on their foreheads jumped out of an alley. The closest one, a beefy brute, threw a punch. Adrian sidestepped and blocked his arm, then swung his cane striking the brute on the side of his face, even as the other man raised a cudgel and brought it down on his shoulder. Ignoring the pain, Adrian turned toward the second assailant and rammed his cane into the man's bread basket, doubling him over.

As Adrian turned back toward the first thug, that brute kicked out and hit the back of Adrian's knees, forcing him to use his cane to maintain his balance, giving his attacker the opportunity to raise his cudgel and catch Adrian on the side of his head with a stunning blow. By now, the second assailant had recovered and was pummeling Adrian's chest and sides with his club.

He felt himself slipping and made a Herculean effort to shake it off. Gripping his cane, he began swinging it between the two thugs, putting all of his body weight behind it, and felt it forcefully connect with each lout in turn, their guttural grunts music to his ears.

Then a shout was raised. "Watch!"

The light from the corner gas streetlamp flashed off a blade one of the thugs pulled from his jacket. Adrian managed to stagger back a few steps, but he wasn't fast enough. A white hot heat sliced through his left forearm. Then in seconds, the two assailants disappeared down the alleyway, leaving Adrian sagging against the building, breathing heavily and holding his aching sides with one hand while the other hung listlessly by his side.

A stout gentleman in a frieze coat, muffler and short top hat, carrying a lantern hurried toward Adrian. "I seen them two ruffians poundin' yer. Likely they wanted to snavel you're purse. Is yer all right, gov'nor?"

Adrian pulled himself upright, setting his world spinning uncontrollably, and leaned back against the building. "I will be in a moment," he wheezed.

"'Course, gov'nor. Did them gallows birds snaffle anythin'?"

"No." With an effort, Adrian straightened, more slowly this time. "Might I beg a shoulder to see me home to Grosvenor Square?"

"Grosvenor Square is it?" The light from his lantern picked up the greedy glint in his eyes at the mention of that prestigious address. "Sure they didn't pinch yer purse?"

Adrian reassuringly patted his pocket, and the watchman leaned in to loop Adrian's arm across his shoulders. Five minutes later, they turned onto Grosvenor Square. As they crossed the alley leading to the mews beside his townhouse, Adrian spotted the dim light of a candle through his study window. The hour was too advanced for servants to be up and about. Certainly none would be in his study, despite that he'd given the staff the night off, knowing he would sup at his club.

Reaching the front stoop, he tipped the

watch with a guinea before carefully mounting the steps and inserting his house key in the front door lock, turning it slowly. If he took the intruder by surprise, maybe he'd learn who was behind tonight's attack.

Noiselessly closing the well-oiled door behind him, he started down the black and white marble tiled hall toward the light spilling from under the study door. He slowed his pace to compensate his unsteady gait. Still, he couldn't avoid bumping into a hall table. The clatter was enough to warn the intruder he'd been discovered. The light went out.

Abandoning any need for stealth, Adrian rushed the closed door, flinging it open in time to see a figure headed for the window. Adrian lunged at him and, grabbing the back of the his collar, slung him around and viciously punched him in the stomach, ignoring the ache in his already raw knuckles or the searing pain in his left arm.

The intruder fell backwards over the arm of a chair and rolled to the floor.

With his good arm, Adrian flipped him over and grabbed the burglar's jacket, raising him to a sitting position. As he drew his fist back to strike again, a weak plea penetrated his murderous rage.

"No, please, no."

With a whiff of the stables, recognition set in. "Bloody hell! Not again!" he exploded. He released her and fell back on his haunches when Paddison holding a lit candle appeared at the study door.

"My lord?"

Lumberously rising, Adrian gestured toward the desk. "Light the lamp please, Paddison." When he looked back, Jossie was stretched out on the floor, holding her stomach, gasping for air. In an instant, he was beside her on his knee. He raised her up, and together they struggled toward the settee where he eased her down and she slumped over, resting her head on the settee's arm.

The butler lifted his fist to his mouth and coughed discretely. "I heard, er, you come in and thought you'd want to know about your other late night visitor."

Adrian glanced at Jossie. "Our friend?"

"Indeed it was, my lord." The formal tone of the butler didn't hint at anything out of the ordinary. "May I get you anything?"

Adrian shook his head. "Thank you, that will be all."

After Paddison closed the door behind him, Adrian staggeringly turned to get a glass of wine for Jossie when she reached out and grabbed his hand.

"Wait."

He turned to face her and she gasped. Gingerly, she rose to a sitting position, with one hand still clutching her stomach, and asked, "What happened to your face?"

He smiled, causing his cracked lip to break open again, and tasted blood. He took out his already bloody handkerchief and dabbed at it. "Got into bit of a tussle."

Her eyes roamed over him before they settled on his left hand. "You're bleeding."

"A scratch."

She patted the seat beside her. "Here." As he lowered himself beside her, she said, "Take off your jacket." She reached up to help him, then rolled up the bloody shirt sleeve and examined the cut on his forearm. She untied the kerchief from around her neck and used it to wipe the blood from the wound and his hand.

"You'd better give me your cravat," she said.

With his good hand, he untied it and handed it to her. "It's no more than a long scratch." She didn't reply, but took the cravat and used it to bind the cut. Under the stable odor, he breathed in her the lavender fragrance of her hair, now mere inches from his chin. Despite his aches and pains, his blood heated with desire, which he tamped down with great effort. "Jossie, what are you doing here?"

She raised her eyes to his and flashed a sheepish grin. "Same as last time."

He frowned. "Looking for more billet-doux." She lowered her eyes but didn't answer. He released a weary sigh. "Lady Bolton is dead, so what can you be after?"

Her eyes met his accusingly. "You were at Vauxhall Gardens the other night."

"Yes, with a party. You never explained why you were in the Rotunda."

Her eyes focused on something over his shoulder. "I was there with Ellen, er, Miss Whiddon."

"Without your chaperone?"

Her chin came up defiantly. "Miss Trundle was with us."

"A silly old woman you walk circles around."

A wave of nausea hit him, no doubt the effects of the pummeling he'd received and loss of blood. He leaned his head on the back of the settee and let his shoulders droop. "I need a drink."

She rose gingerly. "I'll get one for us both."

His eyes focused on the breeches that defined her perfectly delightful derriere as she walked to the console where glasses and decanters were arranged and poured two snifters from a bottle of brandy. When she turned back toward the settee, Adrian said, "Bring the bottle."

She shrugged, picking up the bottle and tucking it under her arm, then carried the two glasses over to the settee. Adrian reached for the bottle and took a long pull from it before he set it on the floor beside him. Then he accepted the glass and waited for her to sit again. "Now, Lady Jocelyn, I'll have the truth with no bark on it."

Chapter 13

Jossie sipped her drink, then coughed as the fiery liquid burned her throat before wrinkling her nose.

"Take another sip, this time savor the taste for a moment before swallowing. It should go down more smoothly," he advised.

Dutifully, she took another sip and swirled it around her mouth before swallowing and was surprised how much better it tasted.

He nodded his approval. "Now, your story from the beginning, if you please."

She heaved a defeated sigh, for really she could see no way out of it. "A young woman has asked me for help. She is being blackmailed."

He frowned. "Go on. What are you looking for?"

"I can't divulge any more, my lord."

"You must trust me, Jossie. There are things afoot you're unaware of."

"So tell me," she challenged.

"No."

"Who are you?"

His expression closed as his cold stare bore into her eyes. "Beg pardon?"

She shifted uneasily to put a little distance between them. "It's just that you have a reputation," she said hesitatingly.

He elevated one dark eyebrow. "Have I?"

She knew he was playing with her. Still, in for a penny, in for a pound. "Yes, as a sinister character. People say you are ruthless."

"Do you find me ruthlessly sinister, Jossie?"

His gaze had warmed considerably as he continued to watch her. Her eyes fell to his lips, and a delicious warmth slowly spread through her. Drat the man, nearly every night she dreamed of the pleasurable heat that engulfed her body when he'd wrapped her in his strong embrace and devoured her mouth with searing kisses as they stood in the parlor at the brothel. With a blush burning her cheeks, she said, "I do not fear you."

His lips curled downward. "You should."

Sitting next to her, he appeared so large, intimidating even, and she understood why he generated fear in people. "You haven't answered my question. Who are you?"

"Adrian Hylton, Viscount Stangate," he shot back.

"No, I mean, how is it you turn up at the most unexpected times?"

"Now you're being nonsensical."

"You appeared just after I found poor Beatrice."

His eyes bore into hers again with that cold

harshness. "I explained why I came looking for you."

"To ask me to drive out with you, which you've never done?" she challenged.

"That's easily rectified," he fired back. "Drive out with me tomorrow."

"Are you asking me, my lord, or commanding me?"

He acknowledged her hit with a single nod of his dark head. "Asking, my lady."

"You've reneged once already," she challenged.

The hard planes of his face softened. "My apologies. It won't happen again."

Encouraged by this small yielding on his part, she continued to probe. "So tell me why you were in the Rotunda."

"Coincidence," he said.

She raised her chin. "Balderdash."

He canted his head even as his lips twitched. "Are you accusing me of stalking you, Jossie?"

"I don't know," she answered honestly while eyeing his bruised face, cut lip, and bandaged arm. "Were you set upon?"

He smiled sardonically. "Yes, but I gave as good as I got for the most part, though the timely appearance of the Watch undoubtedly saved my hide."

She looked at his raw knuckles wrapped round his glass and saw the truth of his words.

"How many were there?"

"Two."

"Were they footpads after your purse?"

He considered this before answering, "I don't believe so. They didn't appear interested in relieving me of my coin. Rather, more like darkening my lights."

Though he didn't add "permanently", she felt the weight of his words.

He finished his drink and stood. "Come, I'll take you home."

"You are hardly in any condition—"

"Don't argue with me, Jossie. You're not traipsing about London this time of night, dressed like that." His hand waved toward her breeches. "I'll hail a hackney."

Without a backward glance, he led the way out of the townhouse and down the front steps. As luck would have it, a hackney stood on the other side of the square depositing its passenger. Adrian lost no time engaging the jarvey, giving him Lady Welbeck's address before hustling Jossie up the steps and into the coach, following close behind her.

A musty straw odor assaulted Jossie's nostrils as the hackney rolled over the cobblestone streets. Through the gloomy shadows offered by the coach lamps, she considered the last time she'd broke into Stangate's study, trying to retrieve Beatrice's billet-doux, and sighed.

Immediately on the alert, Adrian asked, "What's the matter?"

"Nothing," she was quick to answer. "It's only, I was thinking about Lady Bolton. I've felt uncomfortable going about in society ever since her death. I didn't know her very long, but feel responsible somehow."

"It wasn't your fault," he said. "Besides, it's not like she was a blood relative."

"True, I suppose it's because she'd asked for my help," she explained and felt him stiffen beside her.

"How so?"

She hesitated before answering. "Lady Bolton told me someone was blackmailing her."

"Why didn't you mention this before?" he nearly growled at her.

In the hackney's confined space, it felt like he'd turned into a giant vulture looming over her. "No one asked, and I was so rattled finding her, her eyes staring—" She broke off, unable to continue as her mind conjured up the horrible vision.

"No, of course you were upset. Anyone would be," he said in a more conciliatory voice. "Tell me what you remember about the person blackmailing her."

Why would he ask her that? After all, wasn't he Beatrice's blackmailer? She pulled back to get a better look at his expression as the light from a corner gas lamp shined into the coach's interior.

"What's wrong?" he asked, then chuckled sardonically. "I'm not the blackmailer, Jossie."

"I didn't accuse you." Had he heard the uncertainty in her voice?

"No? My dear, your past actions speak volumes."

"I did suspect you, but I don't believe you

are." She released a sigh. "There's very little to tell. After all, I never actually saw the man who killed Beatrice, and she never told me who he was."

The hackney turned into Mount Street, and Adrian opened the window to instruct the jarvey to drive around to the mews. Settling back against the cracked leather swabs, he said, "We need more time to discuss this."

Behind Lady Welbeck's townhouse, he handed Jossie out of the carriage. "I'll come by tomorrow afternoon at four with my curricle," he said, then watched her go through the back gate. He stood there until he saw the faint glow of a candle in a kitchen window. Then, he gave his address to the jarvey and hopped back up into the hackney.

On the stroke of four the following afternoon, Dilhorne announced Lord Stangate, who strolled into the drawing room on the butler's heels. Forsaking his customary black, he epitomized the handsome nobleman nattily dressed in a robin blue clawhammer jacket, a cream satin waistcoat with gold stripes, a snowy white cravat, and tightly fitting, fawn colored inexpressibles tucked into glossy Hessians.

After greeting Lady Welbeck, he asked Jossie if she'd honor him with a drive in the Park. Recognizing his request was a ploy so Lady Welbeck wouldn't guess the drive had been prearranged the night before in the Viscount's study, Jossie gave him a saucy smile. "Allow me time to get my bonnet and pelisse, my lord," she said, then hurried upstairs to do just that.

Thus, a scant ten minutes later, dressed in a dark blue pelisse with matching bonnet, Jossie sat next to the Viscount in his curricle pulled by a pair of matched chestnuts. Little was said as Adrian tooled the spirited team down Park Lane and entered Hyde Park through the Grosvenor Gate and onto Rotten Row. As there was already a great number of people about driving and strolling along the grassy verge, Adrian slowed the chestnuts to a sedate walk.

Turning to her, he asked, "Why didn't you tell me Lady Bolton was being blackmailed?" His voice was gruff, demanding, his eyes snapped with anger.

"It wasn't my secret to tell," she said defensively.

"If I had asked you the reason why those letters were so important, would you have told me?

"No," was her quick reply.

"She's dead, brutally murdered." His eyes held hers. "Think again about your loyalties, and consider that your friend's blackmailer is probably her murderer?"

"That may be true, but—"

"The young woman you spoke of last night who is also being blackmailed, you're aware she could be a target?" He shifted his weight on the bench seat to better look at her. "Your own life could be in jeopardy, Jossie."

"I'll warn her about—"

"You can't protect her."

"No, but—"

"Whoever it is, he must be stopped. Let me help."

Though his tone had soften, his anger was palpable. She shivered, hoping he never directed the full weight of his wrath at her. "I—I'll talk to her about it."

"When will you next see your friend?"

"Most likely at the Marchioness of Rockingham's Venetian Breakfast," she answered.

"Then I'll see you there."

"You received an invitation?"

"No, but it'll be easy enough to get one," he said confidently.

Before she could reply, the Marchioness of Raynham's landau drew up beside them to exchange pleasantries, and Adrian pulled the curricle onto the grassy verge. It was several minutes later before he guided the chestnuts back onto Rotten Row, and Jossie brought up another topic.

"Why did you ask me to drive out with you? I'm not a high flyer like one of your Cyprians."

"Why would I think you are?" he asked, but then his sardonic laugh sounded low in his throat. "Ah, the brothel."

"Yes, that and more," she bristled. "Even though I told you I'd been kidnapped, put in that—that bawdy house to be ruined, you didn't believe me. Rather you thought me . . . easy pickings until you saw me at the Kedleston's ball with my aunt," she accused. "I'm also aware you prefer widows who bestow their favors on you."

He frowned. "How do you know—" He stopped himself from asking as he realized Beatrice had confessed their affair to her. Instead he explained, "At first, I thought you were an actress spinning stories and found you extremely entertaining. I apologize if my behavior was insulting to you, though you seemed to enjoy our kiss." His eyes dropped to her lips. "Do you deny it?"

Jossie's own anger flared when she couldn't stop a guilty blush burning her cheeks. "I refuse to answer you, for you never answered my question last night?"

"What question was that?"

"Who are you?"

His lips thinned, and he took his time answering. "You were a damsel in distress—"

"What does that have to do with who you are?" she demanded. "Besides, kissing me like—like that at the brothel was a strange way of aiding a damsel in distress. What's your explanation for that?"

Thinking to meet his piecing stare with one of her own, she was surprised to see confusion, uneasiness. It suddenly occurred to her that this hubristic and overbearing nobleman resembled a cornered animal. Now why was that? Could he actually care for her?

Adrian focused his eyes back on the road. "It's time to take you home."

Yes, she'd definitely unsettled him, she thought smugly to herself, and listened with only half an ear as he turned the conversation to the Rockingham Venetian breakfast.

It was much later that night while lying in bed before she had the opportunity to review that afternoon's conversation with Stangate and chuckled to herself. So he'd thought she was an actress, which explained why he'd had such a difficult time accepting her story. Also, he claimed he'd been entertained, which meant—

As it hit her, she furiously sat up in bed and hit the coverlet with a fist. That conniving, despicable toad! It was all a sham—his apparent discomfiture in the park when they'd discussed their heated embrace at the brothel—

Well, it was certainly heated on her part! All the while, she'd thought she'd penetrated his tough hide and felt so smug, when in actuality Stangate had out maneuvered her.

That lout had been dissembling to avoid telling her the truth about who he was or what he did. And she'd been naive enough to actually think a single kiss could affect an experienced womanizer like him as much as it had her. Especially since it had been her very first kiss.

Ahhh! The man was a skilled Lothario through and through. That night in the brothel, he'd never believed a single word she'd said. Instead, he'd taken advantage of the opportunity in the parlor to scandalously maul her like the common trollop he believed her to be.

She let anger prevail over the heartache at his duplicity, for she was nothing but a means to an end to him.

Whatever that might be?

Chapter 14

After a fretful night's sleep for Jossie, Sunday presented the ladies a quiet day. Returning from services at St. George's Church, Jossie used the time to catch up on her correspondence, and later over tea, listened to Aunt Cassie try to decide whether to host a card party or musical soirée.

"A soirée would require soliciting entertainment, for I couldn't take the chance that those attending could provide any more than mediocre talent," the older woman mused. "I certainly endured enough caterwauling debutants and inept performances on the pianoforte and harp to last me the rest of my lifetime."

Jossie chuckled. "Unfortunately, I cannot help you, Aunt Cassie, for my musical skills are merely adequate."

"No matter, dear," the older woman said with a reassuring smile. "Being the daughter of a duke quite makes up for such deficiencies."

Monday dawned brightly, the sun high in a nearly cloudless sky, perfect for a Venetian breakfast. A light breeze stirred the ribbons of Jossie's sheer straw bonnet lined with a pale blue muslin that matched her sprigged blue gown as she and her aunt were ushered by a footman to the rear of the Duke of Rockingham's palatial home.

There, extensive gardens opened onto a deep expanse of lawn overlooking Green Park. Tables with elaborate place settings and chairs were arranged under trees and near arbors for guests to enjoy an alfresco repast under tents displayed on long tables covered with a varied assortment of bread, sliced meats, pies, cheeses and myriad desserts.

Ambling among the many guests, Jossie kept a watchful eye out for Ellen. Unfortunately, the first person she clapped eyes on was her cousin Rupert with Sir Percy Carew in tow.

Both gentlemen doffed their hats as they approached. "Good afternoon, my lady, Cousin," Rupert said.

Greetings were exchanged, and Lady Welbeck touched Jossie arm. "I see Lady Kedleston beckoning, my dear. Come get me if you should have need of me." With that, she glided over to a group of women sitting on couches arranged under the shade of a large oak.

"Still keeping company with Lord Stangate, are you?" Rupert's gaze covered the gently sloping lawn.

At once suspicious of his motives, she asked in turn, "What makes you think that?"

He shrugged a padded shoulder. "Stangate seemed overly concerned about your welfare the day I came to see how you fared after Lady Bolton's murder." His brown eyes watched her speculatively. "He's here somewhere as well." He gave her a meaningful eye. "A Venetian breakfast is hardly his usual haunt."

Jossie's stomach fluttered at the mention of Viscount's name. It had crossed her mind while driving in Hyde Park the other day that he expected she'd lead him to Miss Whiddon. And if so, did he have a plan to rescue Ellen? "Nonsense, he's not here to see me." She shifted uneasily and noted how Carew also studied her intently.

Rupert's eyebrows rose, his thin lips turned down disbelievingly. "If you say so, Cuz, though the on dit is you went driving out with him Saturday."

She nonchalantly shrugged a shoulder. "He came by to give me an update on the investigation of Lady Bolton's death."

"Really?" His interest piqued, and he stepped closer to her. "Has the magistrate uncovered new evidence?"

"Very little." For some reason, she was reluctant to disclose someone had been blackmailing Beatrice.

He looked at her for a long moment. "Ride out with me tomorrow, Cousin?"

The last thing Jossie wanted was to be alone in a carriage with her loathsome relative. She could demure, citing a previous engagement, but that would only go so far. Still, she hedged, "Unfortunately, I am promised to accompany Lady Welbeck to see one of her friends."

He bowed his head. "The next day, then?"

Good manners aside, she saw that he intended to pester her until she acquiesced, and so agreed to a time for three days hence. She excused herself and made to join her aunt when someone hailed her. Turning, she saw Ellen approaching on the arm of a well-proportioned gentleman of medium build, russet colored hair, and longish face and nose. She greeted Ellen warmly, who then introduced Mr. Harold Powlett, her fiancé.

His open countenance was pleasing with a smile that reflected in his hazel eyes as he bowed over Jossie's hand. "A pleasure to meet you, Lady Jocelyn." He glanced lovingly at Ellen before saying, "Miss Whiddon has told me so much about you."

The three of them began to stroll toward the formal gardens located at the back of the house. Conversation centered around the Prince Regent's upcoming fête, planned for the nineteenth of June. The celebration was for King George IV's birthday and to show support for the French royal family now exiled in England, though many believed the Prince really wanted to celebrate his new position as Regent. Such a celebration was frowned upon, however, since the Prince's rise in power came about because of his father's mental illness.

At length, they reached one of the many pathways that wound through the extensive formal gardens when Powlett was met by one of his friends who begged a word with him. Jossie took this opportunity to slip her arm through Ellen's and drew her away from the gentlemen and further down a graveled path.

"Without roundaboutation, I searched a gentleman's home who I thought might have Mary Ellen's death notices." She shook her head. "But there was nothing that could be linked to your predicament."

Ellen's eyes were as round as saucers. "Who is the gentleman you suspect?"

"I dare not tell you, though you must know he's asked to meet you and is here."

"Does he know who I am?"

"No, though he'll likely find out since he knows we are friends. But he does not know your secret." Jossie looked over her shoulder to make sure no one could overhear them. "Ellen, you must confess the truth to Mr. Powlett. He will learn the whole eventually."

"No, no," she pleaded, stopping in the middle of the path and grabbing Jossie's arm. "If no one knows, the truth need never come to light."

"Possibly, but you're deceiving your future husband," Jossie argued. "He deserves to know who you really are."

Ellen's blue eyes glistened with tears. "I'll lose him."

"Perhaps, still it's better than living a lie." She reached into her reticle and withdrew a small scrap of lace. "Here, dear, you must not be seen crying."

Ellen took the flimsy tissue and dabbed at her eyes. "I can't bear the thought of losing him," she whispered.

Jossie patted her arm. "Do consider, Ellen, the whole of your life will be spent looking over your shoulder, wondering if someone will recognize you and blurt out your secret. Besides that," she added pragmatically, "if you don't use your real name, you won't be officially married, meaning any children you have will be illegitimate."

Ellen's small rosebud mouth dropped open as she considered the matter. With tears welling in her eyes, she gave a heartfelt sigh. "Very well, I suppose I've no choice."

"Good. Now come, we'll go inside so you can refresh yourself."

Twenty minutes later when the ladies returned to the back lawn, they found Mr. Powlett waiting for them. Soon after, without warning Stangate appeared at Jossie's elbow, causing her to nearly jump out of her skin. He begged an introduction to her friends, which Jossie begrudgingly provided, knowing that his intent was to quiz Ellen to determine if she was Jossie's friend being blackmailed. Fortunately with Mr. Powlett present, no opportunity occurred, and Stangate offered very little to the conversation. He stayed by Jossie's side until Lady Welbeck came looking for her to call the carriage for their return to Mount Street.

As Stangate escorted both ladies toward the front of the house, he asked Jossie, "Will you be home tomorrow afternoon?" At her nod, he took her hand and bowed over it. "Very well, I hope to see you then."

With that, he bid them adieu and left.

On the ride back to Mount Street, Jossie noticed Lady Welbeck's frown. "Is something amiss, Aunt Cassie?"

With troubled eyes, the older woman said, "Jossie, I'm concerned about the amount of interest Lord Stangate is showing you. Even Lady Keddleston remarked on his unusual appearances at social gatherings lately, and then seeking you out."

Truth to tell, though pleased with the Viscount's attention, Jossie knew he meant nothing by it. He was involved with the investigation of Lady Bolton's murder, and since she'd had contact with both of the blackmailer's targets, she was a means to an end and, thus, the reason he singled her out. "It's all nonsense," she insisted. "We've become friends since Lady Bolton's horrid death, nothing more."

"Perhaps." Her aunt sounded unconvinced. "Still, be careful, Jossie, never to be seen alone with him. The gentleman's wicked reputation leaves much to be desired."

While agreeing to heed her aunt's words, she mentally cringed about the lie. She was afraid to even consider what Aunt Cassie would say if she knew how her niece had actually met Stangate. Or the fact that she'd dressed as a boy to break into the Viscount's study—twice now and gotten caught each time. Or the other occasions they'd been together unchaperoned, like the late night hackney ride home and the Rotunda.

Coward that she was, Jossie deliberately

avoided examining her relationship with Stangate for fear of losing her heart. Even today, when Rupert had mentioned seeing the Viscount at the breakfast, her body thrummed, and she had to will herself not to look about for his imposing figure, knowing she was nothing more than a pawn in whatever game he played.

No, she'd do well to ignore the ache in her chest and heed Aunt Cassie's admonition. Otherwise, his inevitable rejection would break her heart.

Chapter 15

It was nearing the dinner time when Adrian met up with Bolton at White's. With the Season in full swing, few were about as most gentlemen would be home dressing for an evening of card parties, balls and soirées. They'd settled at the corner table that Bolton seemed to favor and poured glasses of wine from a decanter in the center of the table.

"I went through Beatrice's things again, and there appears to be several pieces of her jewelry missing." Bolton waved off a waiter before adding, "Also, her abigail said Beatrice had not been herself of late, seemed anxious, jittery."

Adrian took a moment to choose his words. "I've talked with Lady Jocelyn Graydon. It appears that Lady Bolton confided to Lady Jocelyn that someone was blackmailing her, threatening to tell you about . . . ." He didn't finish the thought, seeing no reason to cause Bolton further pain.

Though his eyes wavered, Bolton didn't look away but met Adrian's steady gaze. "Was

Lady Jocelyn able to give you any information, any clue that might help find the blackmailer?"

"None." Adrian toyed with the stem of his wine glass for a moment. "Since the blackmailer wanted information on our troop movements, there's a distinct possibility he is also our turncoat. Have you or the Home Office any idea or suspicions about who might be smuggling information to the French?"

Bolton shook his head. "Other than the usual French émigrés, no. At any rate, I've been temporarily reassigned until Beatrice's murder is solved, so it's unlikely I'll learn anything."

As Adrian's eyes roamed about the room, they settled on the table where Carew had sat with Rupert Malton the last time he and Bolton were here. It was also the night he'd been attacked by two thugs. Could there be a connection? It was something to look into, he thought raising his glass to Bolton. "Should you find anything else among Lady Bolton's things, let me know."

Much later that night in his study, Adrian sat in the burgundy wingback before a cozy fire and reviewed what he knew. Someone had blackmailed Lady Bolton over their affair which was why she'd been so desperate to get her billet-doux back. He shook his head disgustedly, remembering Jossie breaking into his study for the love letters. If only the minx had told him then about the blackmailer, a trap could have been set, and they'd not only have the bloody traitor, but Beatrice would be alive today.

He didn't believe Lord Bolton killed his

wife. He'd a reputation as an honorable gentleman, and he'd taken steps to ensure the sensitive papers he took home were properly secured. Besides, it was obvious he was grieving over her loss and he'd loved her. Bolton was aware of Adrian's reputation at the Home Office, so it seemed natural the Earl turned to him to find Beatrice's killer. But with Bolton being reassigned to another department, the only possible lead left Jossie's friend. And Adrian had a good suspicion who that young lady was.

Which meant he needed to keep a close eye on the enticing Jossie. While that wouldn't be a hardship, it might draw unwanted attention to her if the blackmailer became aware of her involvement with both his targets.

The other problem was keeping his hands off her, and not just to prevent him from strangling the meddlesome minx.

But rather to fulfill his obsession to kiss her senseless.

He shook himself mentally and drank half his brandy in one gulp. She was a duke's daughter, an innocent, and that meant marriage was alternately expected. Not a slip on the shoulder.

No, Lady Jocelyn Graydon was off limits.

He'd better get his head in order and focus on finding Beatrice's murderer and the traitor. Those two objectives should be his only interest for seeking out the delectable Jossie.

~~~~

The day after the Venetian breakfast, Jossie spent most of it accompanying her aunt but returned home well before Stangate's arrival at four o'clock. Having already endured another protracted lecture from her aunt about his sinister reputation as a libertine, Jossie thought it prudent to meet him at the door, and together they descended the flagstone steps to the street.

Then, rather than assist her up into the curricle, his hands possessively circled her waist and effortlessly lifted her up on the bench seat. The smile he gave her as he settled beside her was wickedly roguish.

Once they'd turned the corner onto Park Lane, Adrian declared, "So, Miss Whiddon is your friend who's being blackmailed."

Tempted though she was to glower her indignation at him, she kept her eyes straight ahead. "Is this why you wanted to see me today, to interrogate me, my lord?"

He chuckled. "Back to 'my lord' again?" He didn't say anything else until they entered Hyde Park, and he reined the matched chestnuts into a sedate walk to join the queue of carriages circling the park. "Give over, Jossie," he began cajolingly. "You believe I'm the blackmailer because of my relationship with Lady Bolton."

"I did," she admitted hesitantly. "You must admit the timing of your presence at both Beatrice's murder and Rotunda is highly suspicious." Her gaze met his hard, unrelenting features. "And you did have her letters."

"I gave them to you." His voice was devoid of any inflection. "Despite that, you've concluded I am the guilty party?"

"Surely you can understand why when you consider my view of the events," she bristled. "So far, logic decrees you are still the most likely suspect, especially since you work for the Home Office and know of Lord Bolton's habit of taking papers home with him."

"Why would I want state secrets?"

"To sell for money."

"I'm wealthy and have no need for more."

"You do gamble?" she asked, all too aware of the ruination of many a nobleman because of their gambling obsessions.

"I do, but never wager recklessly. I'm also quite adept with the pasteboards. Have you considered that I was set upon?"

"By some irate husband?" she scoffed, referencing his reputation. Why did this idea rankle so?

His hard blue eyes speared her. "Or possibly the blackmailer himself. Then too, I'm unaware of Miss Whiddon's . . . problem?"

Considering that, she caught her lower lip between her teeth.

She sighed. "Yes, that is a poser. Still—"

"Still, you need my assistance."

She shook her head. "'Tis not my secret to share."

Again, his gaze softened with a look of concern. "Promise you'll send word to me should you find yourself in a situation and need help?"

"I promise."

He turned the chestnuts toward the Park's gate. "I may be away the next couple of days. If anything comes up, send a note to my townhouse. Paddison, my butler, will see that I get your message. Understand."

She recognized his words for what they were, an order, and smiled tightly. "Yes, my lord."

He chuckled and returned her smile with the first genuine one she'd seen that reached his eyes. "I'll accept that for now. We can work on how you address me when I return."

~~~~~

That night, Jossie accompanied her aunt to a drum held at the Russian Embassy in Harley Street by the ambassador, Count Lieven. His wife, Countess Lieven, a leader of fashion, was one of the patronesses of Almack's and a respected political hostess, thus ensuring the event was a crush.

One of the first persons Jossie recognized was the tall figure of Viscount Stangate, his curly dark brown hair easily spotted across the crowded, cavernous drawing room. He stood next to Lord Bolton, the two conversing and, as his eyes met hers, bowed his head infinitesimally acknowledging her, though he made no move toward her.

A short while later, she felt his presence before she turned to find him at her elbow, his piercing blue eyes focused on hers.

"Why am I not surprised to see you here?" he asked.

"Lady Welbeck is friends with Countess Lieven," she supplied.

"I seem to remember your uncle was influential in the House of Lords."

"Yes," she said and added with pride, "my aunt hosted many political parties for him."

"Ah, Stangate, I didn't expect to see you here." An older man with grey-white hair, a prominent nose and soft lips greeted the Viscount with raised eyebrows. "Unusual for you to mix socially, even for a diplomatic affair."

Stangate gave the gentleman a respectful bow. "Lord Liverpool, allow me to introduce Lady Jocelyn Graydon. Lady Jocelyn, the Prime Minister, Earl of Liverpool."

As Jocelyn curtsied, Liverpool's dark eyes took her form in from head to toe. "Ah, you're Allenby's daughter, am I correct," the older man asked.

"Yes, his eldest," Jocelyn answered with a smile.

"Do give His Grace my regards," Liverpool said, then addressed Stangate. "Saw you talking with Lord Bolton a moment ago."

"Yes, we're acquainted," Stangate replied.

Liverpool nodded. "Yes, well stop by my office tomorrow at Whitehall. There's a matter I'd like to discuss with you."

The Viscount bowed his head. "Midmorning?"

"That will do, if not, I'll have my secretary rearrange my schedule." The Prime Minister bowed to Jossie. "Lady Jocelyn, a pleasure."

Jossie watched Liverpool move through the crowd, then turned to Stangate. "Is that about Lord Bolton?"

He made to speak, but a short, dandified gentleman called out to him, drawing his attention. "Forgive me, I'm being summoned by Lord Castlereagh."

"Wait—" But he was already strolling toward a man Jossie recognized as the Foreign Secretary. It struck her that despite Viscount Stangate's absence from the *ton's* social scene, it appeared the political elites knew him quite well.

Though she conversed with a couple of younger gentlemen she'd met over the course of the Season, few people of her age were in attendance. Most were politicians and dignitaries with their wives, many illustrious enough that Jossie recognized them from caricatures in the newspapers or print sheets displayed in print shop windows. Thus, Jossie remained by her aunt's side most of the evening and felt fortunate to be introduced to a great many notable personages.

The hour was advanced before Lady Welbeck called for her carriage. A light drizzle was falling as Jossie followed her aunt down the embassy steps along with others also departing. So it wasn't surprising when a gentleman dressed in a black cloak and hat jostled her until she felt him grab her hand. Her eyes were drawn to her palm as he slapped it with his other hand, then closed her fingers around a slip of paper.

Stunned, she opened her palm to reveal a folded note. Looking up, she searched for the gentleman, but with so many people scurrying for their carriages, she was unable to identify him.

"Jossie, don't stand in the rain," her aunt

called from inside the carriage.

With one last glance along the busy sidewalk, she gathered up her skirts and climbed into the coach. Once seated, she slid the note in the pocket of her cloak, having decided not to say anything to her aunt until she read it.

Some forty minutes later in her bedchamber, having dismissed her maid after being helped out of her ball gown and into her nightrail, Jossie sat before the small banked fire unfolding the note she'd retrieved from her cloak pocket. In bold, slanted script she read, *Unless you want it made public that you spent a night at 25 King's Place three weeks ago, prepare to pay five thousand pounds by this time next week. I'll be in touch."*

For the longest time, Jossie sat motionless, staring at the words. Someone was blackmailing her. But who? Obviously, it was someone who knew she'd been at the brothel?

Only three people came to mind, her odious cousin—though she couldn't prove it, the man who carried out Rupert's dirty work, and Stangate.

She knew Rupert needed money, but would he settle for such a small amount knowing she was worth so much more? She rather thought the greedy toad would make another attempt to compromise her instead. As for Rupert's accomplice, she hadn't any means of identifying him.

That left the Viscount. He claimed to be wealthy, which ruled out his need for money. Furthermore, it made little sense, for if he let out the story of finding her in the brothel, it would ruin her reputation. And since he was the one ruining it, he'd be forced to marry her or risk the *ton's* wrath for besmirching her name.

But that would never happen. For when she'd proposed to him to save her good name, he'd made clear to her he'd bear the scandal rather than wed. So why would Stangate blackmail her?

Then it struck her. This note eliminated Stangate as the blackmailer.

Chapter 16

Jossie had just finished breakfast the next morning when Dilhorne announced Miss Whiddon wished to speak with her. "I took the liberty of putting the young woman in the library, my lady."

Thanking him, she made her way to the library, anxious to tell her about the note she received from the blackmailer, and found Ellen pacing in front of the fireplace.

"Do forgive me for calling so early, but I do not intend to stay long," Ellen said wearing an olive brown short cape trimmed in rose colored velvet and a matching bonnet. "But I received another note instructing me to deliver the money tomorrow night. I am to meet him at Vauxhall again."

"I also received a note last night. Whoever it is, is now blackmailing me," Jossie announced.

"You, Jossie?" Ellen sounded incredulous.

She nodded. "We need to plan a trap for him, or at the very least, identify who he is."

"There's something else," Ellen said, sinking down on the settee. "I told Mr. Powlett the truth." Tears pooled in her eyes. "All of it."

Jossie sat beside her and grasped Ellen's cold hand in hers. "Dearest Ellen, did he . . . break your engagement?"

Tears spilled down her cheeks as she nodded. "He was so very angry," she cried.

While Jossie's heart ached for her friend, she knew the truth had to come out. "Does he plan to expose you?"

Ellen shook her head. "He said he'd keep my secret, only that I must give up the deception."

"What will you do?"

"I don't know," she sobbed, pulling a linen square from the long sleeve of her gown. "Everyone knows me as Mary Ellen Whiddon. I'll have to leave London, go somewhere else, and start over again."

Jossie spent the next several minutes trying to comfort the distraught girl, when it occurred to her that Ellen at least was free of the blackmailer. "Ellen, have you considered you no longer have to meet the blackmailer?"

Ellen dabbed at her watery eyes, then shook her head. "I'm going anyway. I intend to tell him I confessed to Harry, that he's ruined my life."

"Do you think that wise?"

"Probably not," Ellen admitted. "But, Jossie, I cannot let him get away with it, and there's little else I can do."

Biting on her lower lip, Jossie thought furiously. "Very well, let's set a trap? Once we identify him, we can stop him, turn his name over to the Bow Street Runners."

Ellen raised wet eyelashes and stared open-mouthed at her. "Do you think we could do something like that? Would we have to tell them that he was demanding money from us and why?"

"Not necessarily, I could just tell them Lady Bolton told me she was being blackmailed, but not divulge why." Warming to her plan, Jossie scooted to the edge of her seat. "But we need a plan."

As the girls put their heads together, Jossie considered telling Stangate, but then decided against it. He'd never provided a satisfactory explanation for why he'd been at the Rotunda. While she didn't believe he was the blackmailer, she was still reluctant to put her trust in him.

~~~~~

Precisely at four o'clock that afternoon, Rupert drove up to Mount Street in a curricle with a showy team of nervous blacks for their Hyde Park outing. Jossie had considered cancelling but decided to blazon it out, hoping he might let something slip that might indicate if he was the blackmailer.

They'd no sooner settled on the curricle's bench seat when he said, "You've been avoiding me, Cuz."

"As I recall, we did not part on the best of terms," Jossie replied.

"I regret that," he grimaced. "To be honest, I was hurt when you disappeared without leaving even a note."

She narrowed her eyes, staring at him. Did he take her for a fool? "I was taken against my will, Rupert, dragged into a carriage, then forced to drink laudanum and taken to a brothel."

With an expression of astonishment, he stared at her and demanded, "Who would do such a thing? Why am I now just learning of this fantastic story?"

Jossie was incredulous. "You didn't deny this when you visited Mount Street."

"I admitted to making advances when you resided at Allenby House," he replied shamefacedly before he spat out with righteous anger, "You wrong me to think I'd be part of anything so malicious."

She didn't believe his outrage for one moment. Who else would have profited by what happened? No doubt he thought she'd jump at the chance to marry him rather than have her reputation shredded.

"Tell me the whole. What happened?" he ordered.

Refusing to accept his innocence in her abduction, she answered baldly, "I escaped."

"Did you?" His eyes narrowed on her. "How?"

She gave him a smug look. "By the veriest chance, Lord Stangate came to my rescue?"

"Stangate? That libertine?" His frown deepened. "Of course, he'd frequent such an establishment. I suppose that is why he's been sniffing about your skirts."

"Don't be vulgar," she snapped.

Rather than apologize, he asked, "How did you come to meet someone of Stangate's stamp in that place?"

She waved a hand about airily. "It matters not."

"It matters considerably. The man's a rogue, a rake of the first order. If the gossipmongers get wind that you and Stangate were at a brothel together, you'll never live it down. Just being seen alone in his company can harm your standing with the *ton*."

"Fustian! He's accepted everywhere," she argued.

"You should have applied to me. I would have taken steps to ensure your safety."

She gave him a doubtful glare. "The matter's been resolved. I'm under Lady Welbeck's protection now."

"But your home is Manchester Square. As your closet male relation, I should be the one who—"

"Oh, look!" Jossie waved her hand at the occupants of an approaching barouche. "Do let's stop and say hello to Lady Kedleston and her daughter."

Sometime later as they left the Park, Rupert asked, "Have you heard from the Duke about Lady Allenby's confinement? Surely, she will be brought to bed any day now."

His expression of concern, Jossie knew, was more about his self-preservation than her stepmother's wellbeing. For if Lady Allenby gave the Duke an heir, Rupert could be facing financial ruin.

Truth be told, Jossie had not given her stepmother a thought, since there was no love lost between her and Lady Allenby. "I'm sure you'll be one of the first to know," she replied, failing to keep the sarcasm out of her voice.

Rupert didn't bring up her living arrangements again until he turned into Mount Street. "Really, Cousin, the *ton* is reeling with questions over your sudden departure from your home to stay with a stranger."

"None have been addressed to me. Furthermore, Lady Welbeck is my father's sister, which hardly classifies her as a stranger. And for propriety sake, it's better that I don't live with a bachelor." His face flushed with anger, and he made to argue, but she held up a hand. "Enough, Rupert. Let us part as friends rather than adversaries."

"I am not your enemy," he said vehemently.

"Ah, there's Dilhorne waiting for me," Jossie chirped merrily. Before he could set the break, she hopped down from the curricle.

"If I didn't know better, Cousin, I'd think you don't trust me."

She flashed him a cheeky smile. "Why, whatever gave you that idea, Cousin?"

Before he could reply, she turned on her heel and ran lightly up the steps without glancing back.

~~~~

Thursday afternoon, Adrian arrived at Whitehall where he requested to meet with Lord Bolton. Within minutes, a junior office escorted him into the Earl's office and, after greeting each other, he took a seat in one of the chairs before Bolton's nearly clean desktop.

"I met yesterday with one of my contacts who's been assigned to investigate smuggling activities in Exmouth. There he learned that Sir Percy Carew was seen meeting with French émigrés who are reputed to work with smugglers in the area," Adrian began without preamble. "In fact, it turns out Carew's made several trips to Exmouth over the past year."

"Any idea why?" Bolton asked.

Adrian shook his head. "No, but the Home Office has had its eye on Carew for some time now. He seems on excellent terms with the French community here. Another agent spotted Carew and a French émigré with their heads together last week at a pub in Cheapside, setting up a meeting at Vauxhall in the Rotunda. If he were the blackmailer who tried to get Lady Bolton to copy information from the dispatches you brought home, he could be trying to sell information to the French."

"Carew is a bungling fool if he thought Beatrice would betray her country," Bolton asserted heatedly.

"He may be a fool, but he's also dangerous."

"Then you suspect he's Beatrice's killer?"

Adrian shrugged. "It's certainly a possibility, though he never showed that night at Vauxhall. Then again, word is he's completely rolled up," he said. "Rumor has it the bailiff will be knocking on his door any day now, meaning he'll make a dash to the continent, where having French friends would be most convenient."

"Have you a plan?"

"Lady Jocelyn confided to me of another young woman who is also being blackmailed."

Bolton leaned over the desktop. "It can't be a coincidence."

"Too unlikely," Adrian agreed. "However, Lady Jocelyn's reluctant to provide information for fear of betraying her friend. However, I'll keep a close eye on her and the other young lady."

"You know who the other woman is?"

"I do, but again, without knowing details, it would be premature to question her." He gave Bolton a knowing look. "There's no point in scaring her off."

"No, that would be unproductive," Bolton agreed dispiritedly. "You will keep me apprised of what you find?"

Nodding, Adrian rose to take his leave. "With luck, we'll have your wife's killer in custody within days."

Chapter 17

That night, since her aunt was committed to another one of her cronies' card parties, Jossie easily begged off and attended Vauxhall with Ellen and Miss Trundle. Beforehand, however, she snuck into her aunt's bedroom and searched the drawers of a small writing desk and the bed stand, which is where she found what she was looking for, an etched sliver-plated, lady's pistol. The muff pistol was barely four inches and fitted with a sliding safety catch, she was pleased to note. A small leather pouch contained a vial of black powder and five small round lead balls.

Later that evening as she dressed, Jossie chose a dark blue dress with deep pockets with a matching short cape. The weather was turning warmer, so her long black cape would be out of place, yet she still needed the cover of dark clothes to blend in with the shadows.

Careful to conceal the pistol in the pocket of her gown, Jossie hurried downstairs to see her aunt off, then slipped into the front parlor to await Ellen's hackney. She quickly poured some black powder from the vial into the muzzle of the pistol and pushed down one lead ball. Feeling a bit more prepared for whatever might occur later that night, she tucked the pistol and its leather pouch back into the pockets of her gown.

The ride to the pleasure gardens was uneventful, and once inside the girls and Miss Trundle strolled the pathways before settling in their supper box to eat the shaved ham, custards and lemon tarts, and sip the arrack punch.

Nearing the time for the fireworks, Jossie led Ellen and Miss Trundle toward the open area for viewing. As other people gathered about, it was easy work to separate Ellen and herself from the older woman and head for the Rotunda. Just as the last time, several of the lights around and inside the Rotunda had been extinguished, throwing the area in deep shadows.

Walking across the open expanse of the building, Jossie pointed toward a dark alcove. "I'll hide there," she whispered. "This time I brought a gun." At Ellen's nod, she slid into the darkened area and eased the pistol out of the pocket of her gown. With a firm grip on the cold silver handle, she waited with baited breath.

Mere moments later, a gentleman dressed all in black with a broad-brimmed hat pulled low over his forehead entered the Rotunda. Stopping just inside the door, he glanced about and, spotting Ellen, marched straight for her.

"Miss Whiddon," he drawled menacingly,

obviously trying to intimidate the young woman. Jossie noted he wasn't a large man, rather one of medium height and build.

Ellen took a step back closer to where Jossie hid. "Yes. Who are you?" she asked just as she'd rehearsed with Jossie earlier.

He shook his head and laughed lowly. "Do you have the money?" he barked.

"I told my fiancé the truth," Ellen blurted out, her voice shaking with fear.

"You little fool?" he growled, then grabbed her by the arm and reared back his hand to viciously strike her cheek.

Ellen cried out and would have fallen to the floor except for the hold the man had on her.

Without hesitation, Jossie stepped out of her hiding place banishing the pistol. At the same time, a man appeared on the other side of the open area and charged across the floor. He raised a gun and shouted, "Release her or I'll shoot!"

The blackmailer's head swung from Jossie to the other man, who Jossie recognized as Powlett, then turned on his heel and ran for the Rotunda's rear exit.

A shot rang out just as they heard the beginning of the fireworks display. The fleeing figure stumbled, but keep his footing as he disappeared into the night.

"Ellen." Powlett was beside her and folded her in his arms as she collapsed against him. Still in the dim light of the Rotunda, his expression spoke volumes of his regard for the young woman.

Jossie slipped the pistol back in her pocket, released a long breath and asked Powlett, "How did you know we'd be here?"

Ellen raised pleading eyes to Jossie. "Please don't be angry, Jossie. I-I told him you were also being blackmailed. I sent a note explaining what we planned and . . . begged for his forgiveness."

Her voice broke into sobs, and Powlett pulled her to him. "I couldn't let you risk your life, no matter how wrong you were to deceive me. I love you, Ellen. I think you're the bravest of women, to put yourself in danger to prevent a blackmailer from extorting money from your friend."

Jossie cleared her throat. "I'm glad this has worked out for you both, but we still don't know that man's identity."

Ellen lifted her tear-streaked face. "What will you do, Jossie?"

"I'm not sure," she said, biting her lower lip. "For now, we'd better find Miss Trundle."

Ellen straightened in Powlett's arms. "Oh, the poor dear must be frantic by now. Will you come with us, Harry?" she asked timidly.

Powlett smiled and offered her his arm. As they trooped out of the Rotunda, they took the same path the blackmailer used to flee, and when Jossie looked down, she spotted large dark, shiny droplets and stopped. "Could that be blood?" She pointed to the gravel just in front of her, then glanced at Powlett. "This must be the blackmailer's, proof that you wounded him."

"The question is how badly?" Powlett

shook his head. "You certainly cannot meet with that scoundrel by yourself, Lady Jocelyn. Do you wish me to go with you?"

"That's most considerate," Jossie said with a sad smile. "But there is someone who can help me."

"Not—not the man who rescued you before?" Ellen reached for Jossie's arm. "Dare you trust him?"

"Yes," Jossie replied confidently. "I believe so."

~~~~

The following afternoon, Jossie sat at an escritoire in the back parlor writing invitations for a dinner party her aunt planned to hold in two weeks when Dilhorne entered with a folded note on a silver salver.

"This was just delivered for you, my lady," was the butler's explanation when she asked about it. "By a street urchin actually."

Her heart plummeted at the sight of the bold slanted scrip addressing the note. Hoping Dilhorne hadn't noticed her hand shaking, Jossie accepted the the piece of foolscap with a plain, red wax seal.

She waited until the butler closed the door before she broke the seal and read, *Three nights hence, at the south end of the Mall in St. James's Park at dusk. Bring five thousand pounds or else.*

Anger replaced nerves that this was Beatrice's killer. There certainly would be no payoff. Somehow, someway she had to obtain this blackguard's identity. But what was she going to do?

Staring at the script, she came to a decision. She wouldn't go unarmed and meet a fate similar to that of poor Beatrice. What she needed was a better weapon, something more lethal than Aunt Cassie's small lady's gun to confront the blackmailer.

And she knew just where to get one.

Jossie dutifully attended Dowager Viscountess Falmouth's dinner and card party with her aunt the that night. Fortunately, with most of the guests being sexagenarians or older, the partiers disbursed shortly after midnight for their respective beds.

Back in Mount Street, after bidding her aunt good night, Jossie hustled to her bedchamber where Becky awaited her. She yawned loudly and repeatedly asked the young lady's maid to hurry through her bedtime preparations. No sooner had Becky closed the door behind her than Jossie tossed the coverlet aside and made for her wardrobe to grab the groom's outfit hidden inside a bandbox on the top shelf.

Once garbed in the rough clothes, she removed the muff pistol from her bed stand where she'd stashed it and stuffed it in the coat pocket,. Then she picked up her boots and tucked them under her arm. On tiptoes, she left her room, headed down the rear stairs, and out the back door without being detected. It took her a few moments to put on her boots before she made her way to the rear of the garden and unlatched the gate that opened onto the alleyway and mews.

It took Jossie less than fifteen minute to walk to Manchester Square. She encountered little traffic, and of those few pedestrians she passed, none paid her any heed. She kept from looking over her shoulder, for even though nothing appeared out of the ordinary, she couldn't shake the eerie feeling that she was being followed.

Upon reaching Allenby House, Jossie stood on the walkway biting her lower lip while contemplating the irony of having to break into her own home and how best to do it. Finally, she decided to employ the same method she'd used to gain access to Stangate's townhouse.

Sticking to the shadows, she crept around to the side of the house and stepped up to one of the tall multi-paned windows toward the back. She searched the ground for a rock, but found none. She leaned against the cold brick beside the window and wrestled her foot out of the boot, then used the heel to hit the window. Nothing. Taking a deep breath, she took aim again, but this time put more force behind her swing, shattering the small pane.

Holding her breath, she listened for footsteps. When no one came, she used the heel of the boot to scrap glass from around the pane, then reached in and unlocked the sash. It rose easily, and within seconds, she was standing in the middle of the office of the Duke's secretary, Samuel Hardy, stuffing her foot back into the boot.

She felt her way toward the fireplace, where she remembered a branch of candles and flint were kept on the mantle. Fumbling with the flint, she managed to strike a flame and lit the tapers. She didn't have any fear of being discovered as all of the servants but for Rupert's valet and a footman would have retired long ago.

Quickly, she opened drawers of the large oak desk, searching for the key that unlocked the gun cabinet standing in one corner of the office. She'd witnessed her father do this several times, when he'd planned to attend a hunting party. Finding the key at the back of a bottom drawer, she wasted no time in fitting it into the cabinet's lock.

"Who's there?"

The door rattled, as someone tried to force it open. Luckily for Jossie, this room was kept locked, with only the secretary and butler possessing keys.

"Let me in!"

Rupert. Drat the man! He started banging on the door, calling for help. At this rate, he'd wake the entire house. Not bothering to douse the candles, she hurried to the window and hopped over the sill. As shouts were coming from the back of the house, she ran toward the front.

Just as she rounded the corner of the house, Rupert yanked the front door open and, spotting her, yelled, "Got you!" He vaulted down the steps and grabbed hold the back of her coat.

Panicking, she reached in her pocket, wrapped her hand about her aunt's gun, and pulled it out. With a firm grip on it, she swung her arm up and wide, catching Rupert on the side of his head. He let out a howl, but thankfully released her even as two footmen charged out the front door.

Turning on her heel, she bolted down the street. When she rounded the square's park, she threw herself over the fence and hid in the shadows of a leafy bush. The two footmen continued around the Square, apparently not having seen her clamber over the fence. Jossie waited until her heartbeat slowed and her breathing returned to normal before she crawled out of her hiding place and started toward Mount Street.

But her thoughts were in turmoil. She was savvy enough to know she could not forge ahead on her own. She needed help.

Drat! She really had no choice. So without reservations, other than the humiliation of acknowledging she needed his assistance, she slowed her steps as she came upon Berkeley Square.

Chapter 18

After an uneventful night trailing Carew to two low-life gaming hells, Adrian sat by the fire in his study, swirling brandy around in a goblet. It had been a long shot, but he'd hoped to catch Carew meeting with a French contact, all to no avail. Whatever the scoundrel's game, he was playing it close.

A knock sounded on his door. Adrian called out, "Enter," and Paddison came in, followed by a street urchin.

"Begging your pardon, my lord," the butler began, "but Master Robbie has been keeping an eye on Lady Welbeck's townhouse and has something to report."

Adrian gestured for the young boy to come closer. It was hard to tell the lad's age, with a face caked with dirt, ruffled hair matted at the sides, but his eyes revealed intelligence if also trepidation. "Robbie, is it?" When the lad pulled on a dirty blond forelock, he asked, "What do you have to report?"

The lad shuffled uncomfortably from one foot to the other. "Wells, a bloke come out the back 'er ladyship's 'ouse and I's followed 'im just like 'e said." He jerked a dirty thumb behind him at Paddison.

"What did this, ah, bloke look like?"

Robbie scrunched his face in thought. "Small one, 'e were, and in a rush. Couldn't rightly see 'is face though, 'cause 'is cap was pulled down."

"Do you know where this bloke went?"

"Yep, I's followed 'im to one of them big 'ouses in Manchester Square," Robbie said. "Thens I 'ears glass breakin', and whens I's goes to look, I sees 'im climbin' in a winda."

Why would Jossie break into Allenby House? Adrian wondered. "Did you see anything else?"

Robbie bobbed his head up and down several times. "Sures, 'causes I's tried to sneak up, but thens I 'ears all this yellin', and next comes the bloke through the winda, runnin' likes the devil 'isself's after 'em."

Bloody hell! "Did he get away?"

"Yep, but not 'fore this swell comes out the front door and nabs 'em by the collar." Robbie let out a hoot. "Seen the little bloke pull a barker out of 'is pocket and thens wack the swell's noggin, 'e did. Thens off 'e was with two mens on 'is 'eels." A broad smile split the lad's face exposing two gaps for missing teeth. "Beet them too, 'e did," he said with a note of pride.

"So the bloke made it back to Lady Welbeck's?" Adrian asked.

A dirty thumb came up to scratch his matted hair. "Can't rightly say," Robbie admitted. "Los' 'em as I's didn' wants them twos to catch me."

"Well done, Robbie." Adrian turned to Paddison. "You'll see the young man is well compensated for this night's work?"

"Indeed I will, my lord," the butler replied and gestured for Robbie to follow him out the door.

Leaning back in his chair, Adrian took a long pull of his brandy while he contemplated Jossie's motive for breaking into her own home. She had access to it any time she wanted. Besides, she'd been avoiding Rupert. Could that have something to do with it?

He considered turning in for the night, then chuckled to himself as he settled in, wondering if he'd have another late night visitor.

He didn't have long to wait.

A quarter of an hour later, someone tapped on the study window. He placed his refreshed brandy on a side table, then rose and peered out the window to see Jossie with a cap pulled low on her forehead standing on the other side. She gave a little wave, and he shook his head. The chit either had nerves of steel or was incredibly naive.

Or both.

He unlocked the window and threw up the sash. "Generally, my visitors use the front door."

One slender hand reached for him. "Help me over this sill, please."

She thrust a torn and bloodied pant leg

through the window before he grabbed her hand and pulled her into the room. His eyes raked her disheveled attire from head to toe. "What happened to your leg?"

She shrugged. "A slight mishap. It looks worse than it is. A scratch really."

"You shouldn't be out at this time of night, dressed like that," he barked. She was lucky a scratched shin was all she got trying to escape Rupert.

"I can't very well go about dressed any other way this time of night," she replied saucily.

"I ought to strangle you," he said with some heat. Had she so little disregard for the perils that abounded London's streets at night?

Glowering at him, she retorted, "You might consider the difficulty you'd have explaining how my corpse came to be draped across your desk."

His lips twitched at the thought of such a sight. "Would it be draped across my desk?"

She flushed. "What I meant . . . Oh, you're impossible! Let me pass."

As she started toward the window, he held up a hand to still her. "Why are you here, Jossie?"

She huffed and said baldly, "I came to ask for your help."

He motioned for her to move toward the chairs before the fire and watched her roll her eyes before sitting. Taking the matching chair, he waited for her to begin.

"The other night, when I was leaving a drum held at the Russian embassy with Aunt Cassie, a man bumped into me and handed me a note."

At her words, a cold dread settled in Adrian's gut. "This man, what did he look like?"

"I didn't get a chance to notice. I did look around, but he'd disappeared."

"The note, what did it say?" he pressed.

"It was from the blackmailer." Her voice had dropped to a near whisper. "He knows about the brothel and threatens to expose me if I don't pay five thousand pounds." Then she told him about meeting the blackmailer with Ellen and Powlett at Vauxhall Gardens. "Mr. Powlett definitely wounded him though, for there was a trail of blood leaving the Rotunda."

"Bloody hell." He ran a hand through his hair and frowned. "Who else knows you were at the brothel besides your cousin?"

"Rupert's accomplice and Mrs. Dunlap, though I doubt she knew who I was." She hesitated. "And you."

He gave her a wry smile. "So you've decided to confront the lion in his den, so to speak?"

She bit her plump lower lip, momentarily distracting him. Lisette sometimes bit her lower lip in a coquettish fashion, but it never affected him like this minx's innocent gesture. His eyes followed the lines of the loose fit of her jacket, aware of the feminine curves it hid, and her slender thighs displayed in the coarse cotton breeches tucked into riding boots. Adrian's blood instantly heated.

This wouldn't do. She was a debutante, her father a duke. He shook himself mentally. He needed to get control.

"Think, Jossie. It was your cousin who put you there."

Her eyes grew round. "No, Rupert couldn't be the blackmailer."

"Yes, he can." Adrian forced down his anger at her denial as he focused on events around the blackmailer's three victims. "In fact, it makes sense. Malton was probably at the masquerade and saw me leave with Beatrice." When she started to shake her head, he added, "Remember, he had you kidnapped and hidden in the brothel."

"But why would he suddenly start blackmailing people?" she argued.

"His gaming debts for one," he countered. "Then there's the possibility the Duchess delivers your father his heir." As she seemed to ponder his words, he asked, "How do you expect me to help you?"

"Today, a street lad delivered a note at my aunt's telling me to appear in three days at the south end of the Mall in St. James Park at dusk with the money." She looked him squarely in the eye. "Will you come with me?"

He wondered if she suspected that she was walking into a trap, and rather thought she did. That would explain her appearance in his study tonight and her capitulation to accept his offer of assistance. What an unusual creature she was.

"Do you intend to pay?" he asked.

She sat straighter and glared at him. "Never."

"What is it you want me to do?"

"I will be armed—"

"With what?" he demanded.

She reached into the pocket of her jacket and pulled out an ornately carved, silver muff pistol.

"Do you know how to use it?"

"Well, I've never actually fired it," she began, "but my aunt once showed me how to load it and explained it all to me."

"Did she?" he asked sarcastically.

"Yes, she did," she said, miffed. He nodded his head for her to continue. "I want to expose this scoundrel, but I need your help."

"At least you've the good sense to admit you can't accomplish this on your own." He ran a hand through his hair. The minx could give Satan nightmares. "Have you any regard for your safety?"

She frowned. "What precisely do you mean?"

"I mean, Jossie, this blackmailer is also a ruthless murderer. What's to prevent him from slicing your pretty throat?" he demanded.

"That is why I'm asking you to come with me. You know, hide in the bushes like you hid in the Rotunda," she said snidely.

Here was the chance to set a trap and capture Beatrice's killer. There was no way he could let it pass. Unfortunately, there posed real danger to Jossie's wellbeing. But if he and Bolton got men in place well before the dusk meeting, they could nab their man.

He stood and reached out a hand to her.

"Come, I'll walk you home."

She let him pull her out of the chair. "Will you help me?"

"Yes, but only if you follow my directions to the letter." He could almost see the cogs turning in that pretty brainbox as she intently stared at him.

She hadn't yet agreed to his demand when he led her out into the hallway, then toward the front door. He turned a key already in the lock and opened it. Leaving the door unlocked, he followed her down the steps and started walking toward Audley Street when she asked, "What would those directions entail?"

He smiled to himself over her forbearance to ask the question. "That you do exactly as you're told, no arguing," he reiterated. "Otherwise, I can't ensure your safety."

She nodded.

He looked at the sky. "The crescent moon will work to our advantage, limiting visibility." He reached for her hand and drew it through his arm. "Wear a red cloak."

She frowned. "Why?"

"To make it easier for me to keep track of you."

As they neared the mews behind Lady Welbeck's townhome, he stopped and turned to her. Even half hidden under the rim of her cap, her eyes looked luminous in the moonlight, and his awareness of her as a delectable young woman thrummed through his heated veins. Going against his better judgment, he drew her closer in his arms and captured her lips with his.

When she offered no resistance and slowly slip her hands up behind his neck, he deepened the kiss, reveling in the sweetness of her mouth, the softness of her slender form. Her contented sigh brought an onslaught of desire that stole his breath away, and he crushed her to him.

Blissful moments flew by, and so consumed was he in her essence that nothing else mattered except his all-consuming desire for her. Slowly the watch's call registered in his fevered brain, and he drew back and released her. Breathing heavily, he said, "I'll come by in three days to take you up for a ride around four. That'll give you an excuse to be out at dusk."

She nodded, her lips slightly parted. Gathering her to him again, his mouth met hers for a quick parting kiss Releasing her, he pointed down the alleyway. "Go, I'll watch from here."

As she hurried along, Adrian searched the shadows for Master Robbie but saw no sign of the lad. Still, he wondered if the young snoop would report to Paddison of Jossie's return home.

Chapter 19

Saturday evening, Rupert climbed the front steps of Allenby House with some trepidation. Earlier that afternoon he'd met Carew at White's, and over a bottle of burgundy, Carew demanded Rupert settle up the three thousand pounds he owed in gambling vowels.

"In less than a week, I leave for the continent." Carew's countenance flushed with anger, and his dark piercing stare met Rupert's. "Damn creditors are barking at my heels. I need what you owe me," Carew growled menacingly.

"I don't have it," Rupert declared, his own anger rising at being badgered. "Besides, you said you'd wait."

"My situation's changed. You'll have to apply to the Duke," Carew insisted.

Rupert frowned. "Impossible, he's in Yorkshire at Allenby Park."

"Not so," Carew said, leaning over the table as though about to impart a secret. "Saw His Grace's coach pulling up in front of Allenby

House on my way here."

This news sat uneasily as Rupert took a long pull of his wine. With the Duchess expected to be brought to bed any day now, why would the Duke come to Town? "I can't do anything with my uncle here. He's got eyes like a hawk. It'll be impossible to snaffle something to pawn."

"Then you can *and will* apply to him while he's in Town." Carew put his forearms on the table and glowered at Rupert. "Furthermore, the sum now due is five thousand."

"I only owe you three," Rupert sputtered.

"Consider it accumulated interest payments. You'll pay, or the whole of polite society will know you hired a ruffian to kidnap your own cousin and stow her at Madam Dunlap's brothel."

"But it was you who botched it," he charged. "Otherwise, I'd be leg-shackled to her by now."

Carew smirked. "Willa Dunlap let her escape, not me."

"If the truth comes out, you'd be incriminating yourself," Rupert retorted with satisfaction.

Carew gave a careless shrug. "I'll be on the other side of the Channel." He jabbed a threating finger at Rupert. "I want the money within the week. Understood?"

Rupert spread his hands across the shiny surface of the mahogany tabletop. "The only way to lay my hands on that much blunt is to mess with the books, but I can't do that with Allenby here."

"I suggest you find a way," Carew sneered

before draining his glass and putting it heavily on the table. "One week, Malton."

Now, as Rupert entered the ducal mansion, he handed his hat and gloves to the butler and inquired, "Has His Grace arrived?"

Bile rose up in Rupert's throat at that worthy's beaming smile. "Indeed he has, sir. You'll find His Grace in his study."

Moments later, he knocked on the closed door and waited until he was bade to enter.

"Ah, Rupert," his uncle called out with a broad smile, rising from behind the oversized carved oak desk. "Come in and share a drink with me. Watson," he called out and gestured Rupert to a chair in front of the desk.

The butler had followed Rupert into the study and went to a sideboard where he took two tumblers and filled them with brandy. He carried one to His Grace, then handed the other to Rupert before leaving, softly closing the door behind him.

The Duke raised his tumbler. "Congratulate me, Rupert, for my Nora has given me a fine, strapping boy."

Rupert hoped his smile didn't look as forced as it felt. "Indeed, Uncle, an heir at last."

The Duke drank hardily. "Yes, but take heart. I'll do right by you. Can't leave my dead sister's only child without something, eh?"

The knot in Rupert's stomach eased a bit. "That's most generous of you, Uncle." He hesitated the barest moment, but there wasn't going to be a better time to apply for a loan. "Perhaps you could see to an advance? Quarter day is still several weeks away."

His Grace frowned. "How much?"

He adverted his gaze and coughed into his fist. "Five thousand."

"That's a lot of money. Why the urgency?" the duke asked with a frown.

"A gambling debt," Rupert said baldly.

His uncle's frown deepened. "What, you'd best learn to curb your gaming, Rupert." With cold calculating eyes never leaving Rupert's, he eased back in his chair. "I won't be responsible for your debts any more. Egad, at the rate you're losing, you'll bankrupt the Duchy."

"But—but it's a debt of honor," Rupert argued, knowing the Duke understood the time honored code of promptly paying one's gambling debts.

Instead, the Duke made a shooing motion with his hand. "Go find yourself an heiress to marry, Rupert. With your luck with the cards, you'd do better to seek a rich merchant's daughter."

Chapter 20

At St. George's Church in Hanover Square, Jossie sat in the boxed pew beside Aunt Cassie, trying to focus on the vicar's sermon on the necessity of enriching one's heavenly crown through earthly good works. But her thoughts kept wondering to the blackmailer and all the damage he'd done, and how she'd managed to attract all manner of crackbrains for friends.

No, that was being uncharitable.

Poor Beatrice had the misfortune of discovering her husband's infidelity, then allowing her jealousy to lead her into committing adultery. Unfortunately, Beatrice made the fatal error of becoming infatuated with her debauched paramour, Viscount Stangate. But none of that justified her brutal murder.

And Ellen, well, she may not be an adventuress, but the argument could be made that she was an opportunist, scheming to assume a dead woman's identity to mingle among the *beau monde* to acquire a wealthy husband.

Of course, Jossie shouldn't judge the young woman, especially while sitting in God's house on a Sunday morning. Ellen had faced living on the streets and starvation when she couldn't obtain a suitable position. Jossie, on the other hand, came from a privileged family with both money and titles. Who's to say what she would have done if presented with the same choices as Ellen. Even Harold Powlett had come to forgive Ellen's lapse in judgment, perhaps allowing her friend a chance to find a happy ever after.

Then there was her own depraved relative, Rupert, who sought to remedy his financial problems by dreaming up a Machiavellian plot to force her to marry him. Fortunately for her, the womanizing Stangate showed up and contrived her escape from the brothel unscathed.

But with luck, by the tomorrow night Beatrice's killer will be in custody, and Jossie will be free of the blackmailer.

All's well that ends well. Jossie breathed a sigh of relief and, concentrating on the sermon, tried to picture in her mind's eye what her heavenly crown might look like—rather tarnished, she thought.

After the service, they arrived back at Curzon Street to find the Duke's crested coach parked in front of the townhouse. Entering the foyer, Dilhorne met them to take the ladies' hats and gloves and informed Lady Welbeck, "I took the liberty of putting His Grace in the drawing room with refreshments, my lady."

Nodding her approval, she turned to Jossie. "Were you expecting your father?" Jossie shook her head, and her aunt said, "This is certainly unusual. What can it possibly mean?"

They didn't have long to find out. As Dilhorne opened the drawing room door for them, the Duke of Allenby greeted them with a beaming smile and threw his arms open wide. "The best of fortune, my ladies. Nora has given me an heir." He laughed heartily. "The little tyke even looks like me."

Jossie's smile matched her father's. She knew how much he'd wanted a son. "That's splendid, Papa. I've a brother at long last."

"Indeed, indeed! Come, join me celebrating." With that, the Duke called out, "Dilhorne, a bottle of my sister's best champagne."

Once they all were settled with flutes of champagne and small lemon cakes and raspberry scones to nibble on, Jossie asked, "Rupert did not come with you?"

The Duke's smile dimmed. "No, he took it well enough as this puts period to his being my heir, though I'll likely deed one of my lesser estates over to him. Told him, too, he can have the run of Allenby House whenever he's in Town." He leveled her with a steely eye. "Which brings me to ask why you removed here, Jossie?"

Lady Welbeck caught Jossie's eye before she reached for her brother's arm. "For my convenience, Allenby. It is so much more convenient for me to converse with Jossie over the breakfast table about which invitations to accept or decide if we need to make a quick trip to Bond Street."

"What ho!" laughed His Grace. "Never has a female make a quick trip shopping."

Jossie let out a breath and added, "We quite enjoy one another's company, Papa."

"Well, I must say it was a disappointment not to find you at Allenby House. Of course, I'm only in town for a day or two to see my solicitor before heading back to Yorkshire."

"Then we'll plan on you joining us for dinner tomorrow night," Lady Welbeck said.

"Tomorrow," Jossie almost choked out the word. "I'm to ride out with Stangate at four."

Her aunt reached over and patted her knee. "No bother, we'll set dinner an hour later to accommodate you."

"Stangate is it?" the Duke asked. "Anyone else I should know about, Jossie?"

Jossie felt heat color her cheeks. "No, Papa, and the Viscount hasn't singled me out for special attention," she lied even as a tingling warmth radiated through her body with the memory of Adrian's kisses.

~~~~

Later Sunday night, Rupert hopped down from the hired coach in front of Lady Welbeck's and ordered the driver to proceed to the mews behind the townhouse. Though the hour was advanced, the Duke had relayed to him over dinner that the old woman would be at a neighbor's playing card for most of the evening, but his cousin hadn't made any plans to go out.

He was banking everything on that.

After asking Dilhorne if Lady Jocelyn was home, the butler said he'd inquire. But Rupert stopped him. "I've an urgent message from the Duke."

"This way, sir," Dilhorne said and led him down the hall to the library.

"Rupert." Jossie tossed a book aside and jumped up from a dark blue velvet settee. "Why are you here at this late hour?"

Rupert turned to watch the butler leave the room and close the door behind him. "I've come to take you to Manchester Square, Jossie. The Duke had an attack of some sort tonight." He quickly raised a hand to stop her from interrupting. "The physician's been called and says there's nothing to be alarmed about, but it's important to keep your father quiet."

"What happened?" she asked.

"I don't really know as I was out with friends for a good part of the evening. But when I returned to Allenby House, things were at sixes and sevens. It seemed your father had chest pains after eating his dinner." He gave her an earnest look, or as close to one as possible. "Your father has asked for you. You might want to pack a small overnight bag, and I'll take you to see him."

"But his condition—he's not in any real danger," she asked with a troubled expression.

"No, I promise you," he swore fervently. "Still, he dotes on you, and I'm sure your presences would do him a world of good."

"I'll summon Becky to pack a bag for me," she said starting for the door.

"No need for your maid, for it's just for tonight." He saw her frown and, to alleviate any suspicion, quickly added, "You might also write a quick note to your aunt explaining the circumstances so she won't worry."

"Yes, of course," she said, apparently accepting his ploy. "I won't be long."

Rupert heaved a sigh of relief. So far so good. Now to get her into the carriage.

Some twenty minutes later, he heard her giving Dilhorne instructions as she came down the stairs. He hurried out to meet her and took the valise she toted. "Ready?"

When she started for the front door, he took her by the elbow and headed toward the back of the house. "I sent the coach to the mews, not knowing how long it might take you. You know how the Duke hates to keep his cattle standing."

"Very true." She chuckled appreciatively and allowed him to lead her out a rear door and down the garden path to the back gate.

~~~~~

When Jossie spotted the coach, her steps slowed. She was surprised, when instead of two grooms in the Duke's burgundy and tan livery, there was only a single driver, hunched over under a dark greatcoat with his hat pulled low on his forehead. "Where's the Duke's coach?"

"I hired a hackney, thinking it would be faster and easier than ordering the Duke's carriage?" Rupert replied.

Something about this dingy coach aroused her suspicions. "What was all that talk about keeping Papa's cattle standing?"

He shrugged. "Out of habit, I guess. Do hurry now, Cuz. I told His Grace I'd have you there within the hour."

He tossed her portmanteau onto the seat and pulled the steps down to assist her into the coach. After putting them up he hopped in and took a seat next to her. Her unease heightened when minutes later they continued straight on the Great Cumberland Road instead of turning right toward Manchester Square.

"Where are you taking me?" she demanded.

He turned an malevolent eye on her. "Sit back, dear Cuz. We've a long ride ahead of us."

Her anger flared as she realized she'd been duped. "What are you about? Is my father ill or not?"

"No, the Duke is in disgustingly good health," he retorted with a sneer. "Nauseatingly jubilant, constantly talking about that brat who's made a pauper of me."

"When the Duke remarried, you had to know he'd sire an heir sooner or later," she countered.

He shrugged a shoulder. "Since the Duchess kept spitting out daughters, I figured there was still a chance."

"So what now?" She held her breath, fearing his answer.

"Now, you and I make a run for Scotland," he sneered.

She shook her head and said levelly, "I refuse to marry you, Rupert."

His eyes dropped to her bosom before meeting hers again. "Oh, you'll marry me."

His confidence sent a shiver down her spine. Yet, she refused to show him any fear. "Never, nor can you force me."

Glaring at her, he crossed his arms. "After this night, you'll be ruined. No society hostess will have you in her home without a ring on your finger."

"Besides the fact that I don't like you, my heart belongs to another. I'd rather become a shriveled up old spinster than tied to you for life."

"You've not given yourself to another?" When she made no effort to deny the accusation, his chest swelled with anger and he howled, "You'd better not be carrying someone else's welp."

Again, she kept silent. Let him think the worst of her if it would see her out of this mare's nest.

"You bitch!" He reared his fist back and struck the side of her face. "There are ways to handle that," he sneered as a dark abyss settled upon her.

Chapter 21

A soft knock sounded on the study door before Paddison entered. "Master Robbie came to the back door, my lord. I thought perhaps you'd like to talk to him."

Adrian put down his glass of claret as his gut tightened. What reason would Jossie have to leave Lady Welbeck's townhouse at this hour? At his nod, Paddison stepped aside to reveal the scruffy lad who stepped up and pulled on his grimy cap.

"Beggin' yer pardon, milord, buts this ain't about the bloke I's paid to be watchin'. It's that somethin' ain't right," Robbie said apologetically, shuffling from foot to foot.

"What then?" Adrian demanded.

"I seen a coach come 'round to the back gate. It were parked awhile when a bloke brung a gentry mort through the gate and all but shoves 'er in it. 'e was carryin' a case too."

"The lady, did she offer any resistance?"

Robbie shook his matted head regretfully.

"Nay, but she'd asks about some dook's turn-out."

"What did the gentleman look like?"

One dirty index finger swiped the bottom of Robbie's nose. "A swell, 'e was."

"Yes?" Adrian prompted. "Big build or tall?"

"Naw, t'weren't big, 'ad a long sneezer, 'e did."

"Anything else?"

Robbie smiled, revealing his two missing front teeth. "Recognize 'im, I's did. 'e looked like the same gov'nor that yer bloke wacked on the noggin wif the barker the other night."

"You're sure," Adrian demanded.

Robbie bobbed his head. "Seen 'im with me own peepers."

Adrian cursed under his breath as he came to his feet. It was Rupert, and he bet a pony the scoundrel was abducting Jossie. "Paddison order my curricle and see that Master Robbie is well compensated. Good work, lad."

~~~~~

Jossie first became aware of the hackney's rocking motion before she tried peeking through her lashes. At first, she saw nothing but gloomy darkness, then a reflection of a trimmed carriage lamp on glass showed the coach's interior. She realized her face was uncomfortably knocking against the coach's window, making the pounding behind her eyes worse. When she turned her head, her cousin seemed to instantly know she'd come to her senses.

"Awake at last, my dear," he drawled.

"How long have I been out?" Her parched throat made her voice sound gritty.

"Long enough that we'll soon be stopping for a change of horses."

Gingerly she sat up and felt around the tender knot on the side of her face. It was but one more reason she had to escape the lout, for given the opportunity she'd clobber him with all her might before he had another opportunity to beat her. Then, the authorities would hang her for his murder, righteous or not. Maybe she could flee to the continent like a duelist who'd killed his man?

The coach began to slow, and her vengeful thoughts were brought back to the present as he grabbed her wrist in a brutal grip and yanked her closer to his face. "Don't get any ideas about raising a fuss."

His grip tightened until the pain forced her to nod her understanding. He viciously flung her arm away, throwing her off balance, and she grabbed for the back of the seat to remain upright.

Shouts from travelers and the clanging of harnesses heralded their arrival as the coach swerved into the inn's yard. "Don't so much as to utter a sound," Rupert warned as he helped her to alight and led her to the entrance where a battered sign read The Horse & Plough. Jerking her arm, he leaned toward her ear. "Remember what I said."

He threaded her arm through his, drawing her next to his side, and she felt the jab of a gun in his jacket pocket. She allowed him to escort her into the inn, where he instructed the innkeeper to prepare a basket of bread, cheese and a bottle of wine. Pulling her down a gloomily lit passageway to the rear of the inn, he opened a back door that looked out on a privy at the rear of a small dirt yard.

Leaving the door open to light their way, he marched her over to the privy. He released her arm and sneered, "I'll wait here for you."

Recognizing there may not be another opportunity, Jossie took advantage of the necessary. All the while, her mind raced to find any means for escape. As she came out of the privy, the dim light spewing out the opened doorway revealed a border of small rocks around a flowerbed by the inn's backdoor.

Rupert emerged from the small wood behind the privy and started toward her. Before he reached her, she quickly made for the door while untying her reticule, then feigning to trip, she landed by the small rocks. Hunched over, she palmed one hefty stone and dropped it in her reticule as Rupert came up behind her.

He grabbed her arm and yanked her to her feet. "Clumsy, Cuz," he drawled, shoving her through the inn's door.

She felt the weight of the rock hit her thigh and smiled inwardly, contemplating the satisfactory weapon her reticule had become.

Back on the road, with the basket of food on the opposite seat, Rupert sat back in his corner drinking from a flask he'd pulled from his jacket pocket and ogled her person from head to toe.

His slow, lascivious grin sent a revulsive shiver down her spine. It was doubtful he'd wait for the vows before he ravished her, she thought and fingered the stone in the bottom of her reticule on the seat beside her.

She just needed one opportunity.

"Do you plan to travel through the night?" she finally ventured to abstract him.

His glassy eyes met hers and his smile broadened. "No, we'll be leaving the main road before we get to Barnet, after which we'll find a inn to spend the night. Why, are you already anticipating my bedding you?"

"You're insulting," she fired back.

His eyes turned cold. "Tell me, is Stangate your lover?"

His words were like a slap to her face. Still, Jossie remained unflinchingly silent, as her thoughts turned to Stangate's heated kisses. They remained seared in her memory, infusing her whole body with a hungering warmth. But she understood they'd meant only a light flirtation, in fact, were little more than a momentary diversion for him. Another, more sophisticated woman would soon replace her, and he'd leave without a backward glance.

All the while, Rupert stared her up and down. "I don't believe you'll find my love making lacking, my dear," he boasted with a leer. It was some uncomfortable minutes before his eyes turned to the basket.

"Were you blackmailing Lady Bolton?" she asked to distract his lascivious thoughts—and get some answers.

"Blackmail Lady Bolton, whatever for?" His laugh was low, demonic. "Would that I had the chance, though."

"Do you know who did?" she persisted.

He frowned, giving the question some thought. "No."

She eyed him speculatively. "Would you tell me the truth even if you did?"

He was silent for a long moment. "No." He shifted and leaned forward. "Hungry, Cuz?" When she didn't reply, he asked, "Thirsty?" He reached for the neck of the bottle of wine that protruded from the basket.

It was now or never, before they turned off the main road. Taking a deep breath and using all her might, she swung the weighted reticule at his head. Her sudden movement caused him to turned toward her and, before he could react, the rock hit him squarely in the face with a satisfying crunch. Slowly, he slumped forward over the basket and onto the carriage floor, overturning the basket's contents on top of him.

Leaning over, she saw blood pouring from his nose, then reached down to search his pocket for the pistol, which she used to bang on the ceiling to signal the driver to stop the coach. She quickly rummaged through his other pockets and smiled with satisfaction as she pulled out a small leather pouch heavy with coin. As the hackney rolled to a stop, she untied it and removed several gold coins, then opened the door and hopped down.

After tossing the coins onto the roof of the coach, she aimed the pistol at the driver and called out, "Continue on, and neither stop nor look back."

Eying the pistol, he appeared startled at first before gathering the coins and pocketing them as a crafty smile exposed his lack of loyalty for her despicable cousin. "Right you be, miss." His answer was a playful growl, and he tipped his hat at her before slapping the reins on the team's back, moving off at a faster clip than they'd been maintaining.

Jossie substituted the pistol for the rock and put the pouch in her reticle. Pulling her cloak closely around her against the cool night air, she started walking briskly back along the road, its gloomy shadows barely penetrated by the light of the weak crescent moon. She'd hardly traipsed a half mile before the rough road's pebbles and rocks had painfully bruised the bottom of her feet through the thin, soft leather soles of her shoes. With a sigh, she prayed she'd reach the inn before Rupert regained consciousness and came looking for her.

Chapter 22

Past East Finchley, Adrian slowed the chestnuts' pace slightly as he began stopping at the coaching inns to inquire if Rupert's hackney had been sighted. It wasn't until he'd reached The Horse & Plough that he was rewarded. The innkeeper had no trouble remembering Rupert Malton.

"Pretty little miss with him, but she weren't too happy lookin'," he confided to Adrian even before he greased the innkeeper's palm with a golden guinea. "Ordered a food basket, he did and paid up, but weren't no thank you come with it."

After thanking the portly proprietor, Adrian whipped up his team of chestnuts. He estimated he was within an hour of overcoming Rupert's coach and swore under his breath that if Malton had harmed so much as a hair on Jossie's head, he'd carve out the cur's black heart. But first, he had to find her.

As he peered through the moon's dim silvery light at the road ahead, a movement caught his eye. A figure in a long clock darted into the trees. Slowing his team, his eyes tried to pierce the shadowy darkness of the trees to catch sight of a highwayman bent on ambushing him, when he heard his name.

Adrian drew the chestnuts to a halt and tied the reins to the brake. From the pocket of his greatcoat he pulled a pistol and hopped down. "Who's there?"

"Adrian!"

Jossie's cloaked figure rushed out of the trees, and Adrian opened his arms to receive her as she hurled herself at him. He crushed her to him, his heart banging against his chest. He knocked back her bonnet and breathed in her lavender scented hair, her smiling countenance and bright eyes, finally admitting to himself how worried he'd been about her safety.

No other woman had the power to affect him like her. She was constantly on his mind, and all he wanted was to keep her in the circle of his arms. He dipped his head and covered her sweet lips with his, devouring her mouth in a demanding kiss. He couldn't get enough of her. Sanity finally returned when she groaned and raised her arms to his neck. He had to stop while he still possessed some control, or he'd surely ruin her.

He pulled back and, breathing raggedly, asked, "You're unharmed?"

Her hands gripped his upper arms, and her eyes searched his. "Yes."

He sighed with relief and gave her a quick kiss. A shiver shook her body, and he released her to remove his greatcoat and wrap it around her shoulders. "Where's your reprehensible cur of a cousin?"

"Somewhere down this road I suppose."

"I shouldn't be surprised that you got away on your own. Come then," he said, lifting her up into the curricle. "I'll take you home." He untied the reins, turned the curricle, and started back toward London. "How did you manage to escape?"

She pulled her reticule onto her lap and took out a gun.

"You shot him?" he asked incredulously.

Her laugh was music to his ears. "No, I swung a rock at his head that I picked up at the inn where we stopped to change horses—"

"The Horse & Plough," he supplied.

She nodded. "I managed to trip and palm a sizable rock which I tucked in my reticule. Rupert had ordered a basket of food and wine, and after we'd been on the road a few minutes, he leaned across the coach to pull out the wine. That's when I swung my reticule and knocked him out. After that, it was a matter of searching his pockets for this gun and a heavy purse."

Adrian carefully reached for the gun, which she willingly gave up, and slipped it into the pocket of his jacket, then turned an approving eye on her. "Jossie, you never cease to amaze me. We'll stop at The Horse & Plough, get you warmed up and something to eat and drink before we make the dash back to Town." The lights at the coaching inn were in view when he thought to ask, "Do you think your cousin will attempt to approach the Duke, tell him of this night's affair to force your hand to marry him?"

A gay little laugh escaped her. "More than likely he'll be too humiliated."

"Why so?"

"Rupert won't want to be seen in public for several days?"

He turned to her. "You intrigue me. What did you do?"

Her eyes lit up with her smile. "The rock hit him square in the face, and I'm pretty sure it broke his nose."

He reared his head back and roared with laughter. "We'll definitely have to share a drink together to celebrate your handy work, my girl." As he pulled the chestnuts into the inn's yard, it occurred to him that he was actually proud of Jossie's ingenuity in extracting herself from the duplicitous and unscrupulous Rupert Malton.

That thought reminded Adrian of her plan to confront the blackmailer tomorrow night. "Are you still set on meeting on the Mall?"

"You cannot talk me out of it." She eyed him uneasily. "I asked Rupert if he'd blackmailed Beatrice."

"And?"

"He denied it." Adrian felt her eyes on him. "Do you think it will be my cousin who shows up?"

"No."

"Just no?" she asked indignantly.

"Consider that tonight is Malton's second attempt to compromise you to tie the knot," he explained. "Marriage would give him access to your full inheritance, not a mere five thousand pounds."

"Do you know who the blackmailer is?"

He slid the reins to his right hand and reached for her hand. "I've my suspicions. But whoever he is, he's dangerous. He's killed once already, Jossie."

"Yes, and I am not willing to let him get away, not if I can help," she averred.

He gave her hand a reassuring squeeze. "Then we'll proceed accordingly. I'll come for you at four."

~~~~~

Precisely at four o'clock the following afternoon, Adrian turned into Mount Street and halted the matched chestnuts before Lady Welbeck's townhouse. Beckoning a lad with a broad grin to come to the team's heads, he wasn't surprise to see it was Master Robbie. He saluted the lad before setting the break on the curricle, then hopped down and climbed the steps as Dilhorne opened the door to admit him.

"Lady Jocelyn is expecting you, my lord," the butler said as Jossie came out of the drawing room wearing a short, rose-colored velvet cape trimmed in pink satin ribbon over a white muslin gown. The Duke followed close on her heels.

"Ah, Stangate," Allenby called out in greeting. "Won't you come in for a drink before you drive my daughter out?"

"Unfortunately, Your Grace, my chestnuts are a bit too antsy to be kept waiting," Adrian replied.

"Then, you'll just have to congratulate me now." A broad smile split the Duke's lips. "My duchess has presented me with an heir but four days ago."

Adrian stretched out a hand. "Congratulations are indeed in order. Perhaps I can meet you at White's later this evening?"

"Nonsense," came Lady Welbeck's voice behind the Duke. "We're dining later than usual tonight to accommodate Jossie, so you can join us when you bring her back, Stangate."

Adrian looked to Jossie, who gave him a sheepish smile. "I'd be honored, my lady."

"Splendid," His Grace said, accepting Adrian's hand. "Then we'll see you both later."

Seeing Jossie out the door, Adrian tossed a silver coin to Robbie.

"Obliged, gov," the lad replied cheekily before sauntering off.

Adrian assisted Jossie up into the curricle and watched her settle on the curricle's bench seat, carefully placing her reticule on her lap. Sitting beside her, he took up the reins, released the brake, and guided the chestnuts into the road. "The Duke is obviously pleased with his heir," Adrian said as he tooled the team toward St. James's Park.

Jossie smiled. "Yes, and it is grand to think I've a little brother."

"Have you plans to go to Yorkshire soon?"

Her smile dimmed. "Not until after the Season. Even then, I'm not sure if the Duchess will welcome me, but I intend to go anyway."

Perceiving her remark touched on the Duchess's dislike for her step-daughter, Adrian, noticing her attire, changed course and asked, "No red cloak?"

She shook her head. "I don't own one, and didn't want to raise questions by asking Aunt Cassie to lend me hers."

"Fair enough." He glanced at her reticule. "Is Lady Welbeck's handgun in your reticule?"

"Yes." She sat up straighter bristling. "I feel I should have something on my person to protect myself."

He held out his hand. "Please hand it to me."

She ignored his command. "It has a safety latch."

"Still, you're not familiar with firearms." He gestured with his open palm for the gun.

She glanced at his hand and raised pleading eyes to his. "I had Rupert's last night."

"You took it off of him after you knocked him unconscious," he countered.

"Please, if something should go wrong—"

"You've my word, nothing will."

"But should it," she persisted. "At least I'll have the gun to protect myself. He—he might coerce me to leave with him.

"It will be over my dead body," he swore under his breath. She'd be within his sight the entire time.

"You just proved my point." She drew a deep breath. "Should something go awry, I will at least have a weapon to use against him."

Adrian heard the near panic in her voice and understood the sense of security the small pistol gave her. He divided the reins between both his hands again. "You'll keep the safety on while it's in your reticule?" She nodded, and he felt he had to be satisfied with that. "This is a bad start to keeping your promise to do exactly as I say."

With a rueful smile, she replied, "It won't happen again."

"We'll be arriving well before dusk which will afford plenty of time for me to get into position before the blackmailer comes." Jossie nodded her head. "You will stay out in the open, and not let him lead you anywhere."

"What if—"

"There is no 'what if'," he said between gritted teeth. "Should he manage to get you in a secluded area, there's no telling what he might try." When she gave him another nod, he growled, "I expect you to keep to the plan."

Swinging around to look at him, she declared, "And I expect you to treat me as an equal in this. I'll do my part, but I won't jeopardize letting him get away for killing Beatrice *if* it means I must deviate from your plan."

Adrian drew a deep breath to clamp down his anger. "No heroics, Jossie. This man is dangerous. You've my word, he will not escape."

She frowned. "What guarantee can you provide?"

He and Bolton already had men stationed about the park. But he hesitated telling her in case somehow her actions should give it away. "Trust me, Jossie."

"I came to you, Adrian." Her shoulders relaxed, and she looked down at her clenched hands in her lap. "I do trust you." Raising her eyes to his face, she asked again, "Do you know who the blackmailer is?"

"I told you, I've my suspicions," he hedged.

"Rupert?"

"It would seem likely since he tried to kidnap you twice now, but there is another man I've been investigating. We're almost there," he said to prevent further discussion.

The curricle soon turned into St. James's Park. At this hour, there were a substantial number of people and equipages going up and down the Mall, a wide open park area with trees along the edges. Adrian took a trail leading to the park's lake and pulled the curricle onto the verge. It wasn't long before a young lad appeared to take the horses' heads, and Adrian helped Jossie down. After giving the lad instructions to keep the chestnuts quiet and a promise of a gold coin, he took Jossie's arm and led her back toward the Mall.

When they reached the Mall, he held back. "You will walk up and down in plain sight, but stay nearer these trees at all time. I'll be hiding among them, watching closely. But under no circumstance must you look for me, understand?"

She nodded and looked out on the Mall, which was slowly emptying of people, then back at him. He thought he saw fear dim her silver grey eyes, but it was gone in a moment. He took her hand and raised it to his lips. "Have faith in me, Jossie. I swear on my life, I'll let nothing happen to you."

Chapter 23

Jossie did have faith in Adrian. While sitting beside him in the curricle, she knew it was more than his tall muscular physique and broad shoulders that lent her comfort. He'd been her dark knight in shining armor ever since he'd first rescued her from the brothel. Even then, as his piercing blue eyes hinted at danger, she knew he could be compassionate. "Who are you?" Jossie suddenly demanded, realizing he'd always evaded the question.

He trained his steely glance on her. "Someone you don't want for an enemy, Jossie."

Ahhhh! She heard the menace in his voice and understood he'd earned his sinister reputation. A cold shiver ran down her spine. Yet despite the minatory threat of his presence, his nearness comforted her, though she did wonder why he bothered to spend time with her, much less coming to her rescue each time she landed in trouble.

He left her then, striding purposefully

back down the lane toward the curricle. Slowly, she turned and ambled around the Mall which, because of the hour, was quickly thinning of people. Glancing up at the lowering sun, she estimated she hadn't long to wait for the blackmailer to make himself known.

That thought had barely left her when a figure in a dark firenze coat with a black, wide-brimmed hat pulled low on his forehead stepped in her path, took her arm in a vice-grip to swing her about to walk beside him.

"Not a sound or it'll be your last," the man hissed.

She looked up into dark eyes, noting his small mouth and rounded, weak chin that seemed to disappear into the high points of his collar and cravat, and bit her bottom lip to keep from calling out as she recognized Sir Percy Carew. Her eyes darted about wildly, but the few people about were some distance from them. "What do you want?" The tremble in her voice angered her, and she inhaled deeply to boost her courage. "Why are you doing this?" she demanded more forcefully.

"Keep walking," he said, jerking her closer to his side. "Think I didn't see you arrive with Stangate?" Her eyes flew to his face as he sneered down at her. "Oh yes, I was watching," he taunted.

Where was Adrian? She tried to hold her panic down. Did he have enough time to get into place? Was he watching them even now as Sir Percy dragged her toward a black coach waiting up ahead? She considered trying to retrieve the pistol from her reticule, but before she could act on it, a shout rang across the Mall. "Halt or I'll shoot!"

Immediately, Carew swung her around and used her as a human shield to face Stangate who held a gun by his side, confidently striding across the Mall toward them. At the same time, she felt a jab in her ribs and knew instantly that Carew had pulled a gun from his pocket.

"Stay where you are, Stangate," Carew called out.

Steadily advancing on them, Stangate ordered, "Let the lady go."

"Or what?" Carew's threatening laugh went through her like a cold fission, making her stomach convulse in fear. "No, the game is mine. Stop where you are or I fire."

Stangate drew to a halt not twelve paces from them. "You won't leave this park alive if you do. Let her go."

"And make myself a sitting duck," Carew scoffed wrapping his arm around Jossie's waist and drawing her more tightly against his body. "No, we play the hand my way. The lady will leave with me in the hackney. I'll release her the moment we are out of the park, provided we're not followed."

"What hackney?" Stangate asked.

Carew jerked Jossie as he turned slightly to look over his shoulder. At the same moment in one fluid motion, Adrian stepped to the opposite side, giving him a clearer shot at Carew's head, brought his hand up and fired.

Jossie screamed over the deafening roar of Stangate's gun as a warm red liquid splattered the side of her face and ran down the front of her velvet mantle. Carew's hold on her loosened as he started to sink toward the ground, taking her with him. Then, she was wrenched from his lifeless arm and wrapped in a tight embrace against Adrian's broad chest.

"Hush, hush, Jossie," he said reaching up with his handkerchief to wipe Carew's blood off her cheek. "I've got you. All is well."

"Ohhhh." The ringing in her ears was deafening, and she couldn't stop wailing, clinging to the front of his jacket. He rocked her gently, crooning over and over, "It's over. You're unhurt. Easy, Jossie."

Gradually her cries settled to wrenching sobs as it vaguely registered that other men were running about shouting orders. A man who looked like Adrian's butler stood beside him and said something to Adrian while gesturing toward the entrance of the Mall.

Adrian pulled away, and instantly she was cold, bereft of his embrace. "Look at me, Jossie," he ordered giving her a small shake. "Look at me."

Drawing in a shuddering breath, she managed to stop whimpering but found she was so cold her teeth started chattering. Adrian pulled her to him again, rubbing her back, then picked her up and carried her toward a coach that was coming down the Mall toward them. The driver had barely stopped when another man—Lord Bolton!—stepped up and opened the door.

Lord Bolton's eyes met Adrian's, and a silent agreement passed between the two men. They nodded to one another before Adrian hopped in the coach with Jossie still in his arms. He sat with her on his lap. "I'm taking you to your aunt's, Jossie, and sending for a doctor. You're experiencing shock. I'm sorry I had to end it that way. I hope you can forgive me."

"F-forgive y-you?" He'd killed Carew while the man held her. His head had been inches from hers. Carew's blood ran down her face, stained her cape. Oh heavens, a dead man's arm embraced her. "You s-shot him—in the head."

"Don't let your mind dwell on it," he said, obviously seeing her relive the horror in her eyes. He untied the ribbon of her bonnet and tossed it on the opposite seat. One side was splattered in blood.

"My head was next to his." She heard the hysteria in her voice. "His b-blood, his blood is all over me." She stared wide-eyed at him, bile tickling the back of her throat. "It could have been mine."

"I never miss, Jossie."

"W-What!" she stuttered on a sob. She was so cold, her whole body shivered.

He pulled her head against his shoulder. "Hush, Jossie." With one arm securely around her, he began searching the several small compartments until pulling a sliver flask from one, saying "Ah, good man Bolton."

He unscrewed the lid, sniffed the contents,

and held it to Jossie's lips. "Take a sip, hold it in your mouth for a few seconds before you swallow." When she made to refuse, he growled, "Do it, Jossie. It'll help warm you."

Reluctantly she did as he ordered and sipped the vile tasting whisky, holding it in her mouth a moment before swallowing. She coughed as it burned its way to her nauseous stomach.

"Another," Adrian ordered, forcing her to accept several more mouthfuls.

Though the burn was as great as the first swallow, she didn't cough. She began to feel the whisky's effects and relaxed slightly in the comfort of his arms, leaning against his chest.

"Jossie," he whispered, pressing a kiss to her forehead, "I can't do this any longer."

She looked up and was surprised by his troubled eyes. "W—what do you mean?"

"Granted, I had no control over your cousin's actions," he said. "But Carew I knew about. He was a suspected traitor I was investigating for the Home Office. From the moment you met me, you've been exposed to any number of dangerous situations—life threatening even."

"You didn't cause them," she defended weakly.

"No, but I court danger." He shook his head. "If anything had happened to you back there, I wouldn't be able to live with myself." He stroked her hair and gently pulled her head to his shoulder. "I know you're aware of my reputation as a libertine, a ruthless gambler, a dangerous wretch when crossed."

Yes, but never with me. She swallowed back a cry. "I know you—"

An index finger pressed against her lips to silence her. "You think you know me. The truth is I'm all of those things, and worse." He leaned over and brushed his lips across hers, gently at first, then took possession of them, slowly deepening the kiss.

A comforting languor seeped into her veins, and Jossie gave herself over to it just before the coach came to a stop. They'd arrived at Mount Street. When he raised his head, he whispered, "For your welfare and my sanity, this must be farewell."

~~~~

Adrian intended to stay only long enough to order Dilhorne to send for a physician. But as he stood in the front hall with a protective arm about Jossie, the Duke came out of the drawing room.

"Damnation!" Jossie's father blustered. "Was there an accident? Where is she hurt?"

"She's not physically hurt," Adrian began and released his hold on Jossie. He was forced to quickly replace it about her wobbling figure. "She's experienced a disturbing event and is in shock. I've requested Dilhorne to send for the physician."

"Then go, man," the Duke ordered the butler.

Lady Welbeck came out of the drawing room and hurried toward the door. "Good heavens! All that blood."

"Ooooh," Jossie moaned, bringing a hand up to her lips, as she lost what little color the whiskey had brought to her cheeks.

Scooping her up in his arms, he said to her aunt, "Lead me to her bedchamber?"

Lady Welbeck nodded her head and turned toward the stairs, calling orders to a footman coming from the back of the house. "Send Lady Jocelyn's maid to her bedchamber and have a warm bath prepared."

Adrian gently laid Jossie atop the counterpane of a four-poster bed. Bending over her, he smoothed damp locks off her cheek and whispered, "Goodbye, Jossie. Take care of yourself." He said nothing about seeing her again. Instead, he turned and walked out of her room—out of her life—to return downstairs where Dilhorne informed him His Grace requested a word with him.

Ushered into the study, Adrian was greeted with a glass of brandy by the Duke, who instructed him to explain why his daughter was covered in blood.

After giving a somewhat abbreviated account of events that led up to Carew's death, Adrian concluded with the observation, "Lady Jocelyn attracts trouble like a moth drawn to a flame, Your Grace."

The Duke was not appeased with Adrian's report and, instead, took the time-honored parental stance about his daughter's reputation. "If it's as you've said, you've been meeting my daughter surreptitiously for weeks," the Duke accused with an angry glare. "Are you prepared to protect her from the ensuing scandal?"

"You've my word, no scandal will be attached to her name," Adrian assured the angry nobleman.

"But if there is—"

"We'll cross that bridge when we come to it," Adrian interjected coming to his feet to bid the Duke adieu.

Chapter 24

Jossie wasn't given any time to contemplate Adrian's words, for Becky arrived on his exit and prepared her for a hot bath, then saw her tucked in bed just as the physician arrived.

He could find nothing wrong except for the bruise on her cheek, from when Rupert had struck her the night before, and overset nerves. After leaving a small dose of laudanum to help her sleep, he professed she'd feel more herself by the following morning.

But alas, that wasn't the case. Adrian failed to make an appearance that day. Instead, mid-morning she received a note from Lord Bolton, saying he would come later in the afternoon with the magistrate, Sir John Fielding, who needed to question her about the events leading to Sir Percy's death.

When both gentlemen arrived at three, Jossie's aunt sat beside her on the settee in the drawing room. "To give my niece moral support," the older woman told both gentlemen.

Sir John was quick to assure Lady Welbeck he was simply tying up loose ends, and Bolton insisted it was a mere formality, that Jossie had nothing to fret over, especially as he would remain with her throughout the interview.

But before the magistrate could pose the first question, Dilhorne announced the Duke of Allenby.

Pulling up short just inside the doorway, His Grace exclaimed, "What's this? What brings you to my sister's home, Sir John?"

"I'm glad you're here, Your Grace," Lord Bolton said, coming to his feet. "This is a matter that Lady Welbeck should well be spared."

"But not my daughter?" the Duke blustered. "Here now, what's all this?"

"If you will, Your Grace," Sir John said, nodding to Aunt Cassie. "Lady Welbeck, you may retire if you like."

The older woman took a moment to study each man's grim countenance, then looked at Jossie, who gave her a weak smile. "Since I'm already aware of the details, and your father is here, I believe I will." With that, she patted Jossie's cheek. "Take heart, child. All will go well, now that the Duke is here."

After Lady Welbeck left, Jossie resumed her seat on the settee with her father sitting next to her. "Now, gentlemen, what's this about?" he demanded with ducal authority. He listened to Lord Bolton give a concise summation of events leading up to Carew's death, though he didn't seem surprised by any of it. Jossie wondered what exactly Adrian had divulged to her father when he turned and asked, "Are you up to this inquisition, Jossie? For if not—"

"Please, Papa," she said, "it's best to do it now and get it over with."

He nodded approvingly and ordered, "Then proceed, Sir John."

The magistrate cleared his throat. "No one has explained why were you being blackmailed, Lady Jocelyn."

"What?" His Grace howled, making Jossie jump in her seat. His blue gaze impaled her. "Stangate never mentioned that."

"My lady," Lord Bolton said, coming to his feet to take a chair next to her. "Viscount Stangate told me a little of the predicament in which he found you. You have my assurance that whatever is revealed today will go no further than this room. The details are not pertinent for Sir John's investigation, and your presence can be left out of the official report." He leveled his eyes on the magistrate. "Is that not so, Sir John?"

The magistrate met Bolton's forthright stare. "You're saying the reason for Carew blackmailing this young woman has little bearing on his death?"

"It has none," Bolton averred. "Carew was being investigated by the Home Office and proven to be a traitor. He was killed by an agent of the Crown, and his demise will greatly impede a band of smugglers around Exmouth. So Lady Jocelyn's role is auxiliary in bringing Carew to justice."

"Exmouth?" Jossie asked, her eyes widening with revelation. That might explain how Carew knew Ellen wasn't Miss Whiddon if he saw her there with Baron Aylesbeare and his family.

Lord Bolton looked at Jossie. "Is something wrong, Lady Jocelyn?"

She waved his question aside. "Oh no, it's just that I have a friend who came from there. That is all."

With his sharp gaze on Jossie, Sir John pursed his lips together. "I'll hear your story now, Lady Jocelyn, before making any definite decisions."

Jossie supposed she'd have to be satisfied with that. She drew in a deep breath and cut a sheepish glance at her father before replying, "My cousin proposed to me, but when I refused, he had me kidnapped and placed in a brothel in the hope it would ruin me, thereby forcing me to marry him. It's my belief that Carew was involved somehow, since he was in possession of the details."

"Rupert's a dead man," the Duke swore under his breath in the prolonged silence that met her claim. For a fleeting moment, Jossie actually felt sorry for Rupert, knowing her father would not let her cousin's actions go unpunished.

"Go on," Sir John encouraged. "What happened yesterday on St. James's Mall?"

Jossie proceeded to describe Adrian's plan, with Lord Bolton adding that agents had been stationed around the entire park to prevent Carew's escape.

"What went wrong?" Sir John asked

Jossie.

"Carew had hired a hackney and tried to drag me to it. That's when Lord Stangate appeared with a gun and started toward us, demanding Carew release me. Carew refused and, instead, held me in front of him like a shield, and then . . . Lord Stangate shot him in the head."

"Damnation!" the Duke exclaimed.

Sir John frowned. "His head, it was next to yours? That was why you were covered in blood?"

Jossie nodded.

"I've heard some claim Stangate a soulless brute," His Grace said with deference.

"Must have nerves of steel," the magistrate added.

Lord Bolton cleared his throat. "Stangate is a superb shot."

"He never misses," Jossie agreed softly, repeating Adrian's own words.

"I must say, quite the ordeal for a young lady to experience. I applaud your bravery, Lady Jocelyn." Sir John nodded once, then turned to Bolton. "The official report will state that Carew was trying to escape capture from officers of the Home Office for the charge of treason. Viscount Stangate came upon him and was forced to fire at Carew when the traitor drew his gun on him."

"Thank you, Sir John," Bolton said. "But for security reasons, the Home Office doesn't want Carew's traitorous actions made known. For public knowledge, another version will be put about for Carew's sudden death."

Sir John raised one disbelieving eyebrow. "Do you agree with this, Your Grace?"

The Duke was quiet for a long moment, studying Bolton. "I assume the Prince Regent is aware of Carew's actions?"

Bolton hesitated for the barest second. "Something along the report that Sir John will write up, yes."

"Will this satisfy you, Jossie?" His Grace asked.

She could only nod, as relief flooded through her that the whole blackmailing ordeal was finally over.

"Very well," the Duke concurred.

Lord Bolton and Sir John didn't linger, and no sooner had Dilhorne shown the two gentlemen out than His Grace rounded on Jossie. "Now, young lady, you've some explaining to do. Am I correct to assume you're staying with Cassie because you were not safe in your own home?"

Jossie nodded. "I had no other place to go."

"Stangate, did he compromise you in any way at that brothel? Cassie said he's been singling you out at events. Even I've met him here coming for you." His blue eyes narrowed as he studied her face.

She silently cursed the heat that seared her cheeks. "A kiss only, Papa." *Well, it wasn't just a kiss*, she amended mentally. *It was toe-curling, heart stopping, as were the others*.

For several long moments, she withstood his piercing scrutiny before he demanded, "You'd tell me if he crossed the line?"

More like she'd been the one who'd crossed the line, thrice by her reckoning beginning with breaking into his study dressed as a boy, she thought ruefully. "I would, Papa."

He nodded, seemingly satisfied, then gave her a fond smile as he put an arm around her shoulders and drew her into his side for a hug. "I'm proud of you, Jossie. By all accounts, you were instrumental in bringing that turncoat Carew to justice."

The drawing room door opened, and Lady Welbeck entered and, seeing father and daughter ensconced on the settee, smiled. "I presume all is well?"

"Indeed," His Grace said. "Jossie may return home at any time. Rupert is banished permanently from the Allenby House."

"Really, Papa, I'm quite content here," Jossie protested. "Aunt Cassie and I rub along together quite well, and as she is my chaperone, staying here is more convenient for both of us."

"Don't upset the apple cart, Allenby," his sister cautioned him.

"Very well," he conceded, "since I plan to leave tomorrow for Yorkshire anyway, I suppose there's no hurry for Jossie's return."

"You'll stay for dinner?" Lady Welbeck asked.

His Grace eagerly accepted, making Jossie groan inwardly, knowing he'd probe for more details pertaining to the brothel and other events better left alone.

The following morning, Aunt Cassie pointed out an obituary in *The Times* that stated Sir Percy Carew had unexpectedly succumbed to what his physician, Dr. Samuel Capers, ascribed to be an extreme case of food poisoning. Sir John had kept his word, with not a hint of her involvement, or Adrian's for that matter, in the scoundrel's death.

Days passed without Adrian putting in an appearance, and Jossie felt heartsick. Remembering his last words, she feared of never having the opportunity to dispute his claim that it was his very presence that had put her in jeopardy. Silly man, surely he deduced she'd been the catalyst for all the troublesome predicaments she'd landed in. Truth was, he'd been her knight in shining armor rescuing her each time.

Nor could she tell him how much she cared for him—loved him.

At the end of a long, lonely week, Jossie attended a musical evening with her aunt where she met up with a smiling Ellen, accompanied by Harold Powlett.

"Oh, Jossie, I'm so happy," the lovely blonde gushed, greeting Jossie at the refreshment table. "Harry has completely forgiven me. We're to marry in one month's time."

"That's wonderful." Jossie did share in Ellen's joy, glad that Carew had not destroyed another woman's life. When Powlett's attention was drawn by another guest, Jossie pulled Ellen aside. "Forgive me for asking, Ellen, but how will you explain your alias to the *ton*?"

"Harry came up with the perfect idea." Ellen lowered her voice. "He suggested I go on as before since after the wedding, which will be small and private, I'll be Mrs. Powlett. That way, no one need ever know of my—my deception."

Applauding Mr. Powlett's astute handling of Ellen's situation, Jossie promised to attend the couple's nuptials.

Over the course of the next week, Jossie looked for Adrian at the routs and soirées she and her aunt attended, but he never put in an appearance. At Almack's on Wednesday night, Lady Jersey pointedly commented to her about Adrian's absence on the social scene.

"I had thought he'd show tonight, knowing you'd be here, Lady Jocelyn," the patroness speculated baldly. "It was you, after all, who brought the elusive Viscount out of the shadows."

On Thursday, she'd applied to her aunt to attend the Barb's *Hamlet* at the Drury Lane Theatre, where she thought he might appear with his mistress. John Philip Kemble admirably portrayed the haunted Danish prince, and Jossie did see Adrian's former mistress. Her brunette tresses sported two ostrich plumes while a diamond necklace drew the eye to the low décolletage of her gold crepe gown as she hung on the arm of an older and rather stout gentleman. But Adrian's dark head and broad shoulders remained absent.

Seeing Jossie's eyes straying repeatedly to the attractive brunette's box, Aunt Cassie leaned toward her and whispered, "I'm sorry, my dear.

You deserve so much better."

Nor did she catch a glimpse of his curricle traversing the streets of Mayfair or tooling around Hyde Park. He'd simply vanished altogether from the social scene.

Thus on Friday, nearly two weeks after Adrian had bid her goodbye, Jossie expressed her desire to stay home rather than spend another fruitless evening searching for the man's broad shoulders and dark head of hair at Lady Kilpatrick's soirée.

Hearing this, Aunt Cassie tsked. "I did try to warn you not to read too much into the attention Stangate paid you, my dear. The man's an unrepentant libertine, and it's well known a tiger doesn't lose its stripes." Relenting somewhat, she patted Jossie's hand. "Very well, we can skip tonight, for no doubt Nelly Kilpatrick has invited the whole of London, and we'll not be missed."

At dinner, Jossie had little appetite and picked at her food, rearranging it on the plate. Afterwards, the ladies retired to the cozy back parlor where Jossie left her aunt reading by the fire to let herself out onto the rear terrace, and looked out over the garden bathed in the silvery light of a half-moon.

Her heart ached over Adrian's defection, but she'd only herself to blame. After all, he never made any promises, in fact, had repeatedly warned her about his roguery.

A balmy breeze ruffled the leaves of an oak tree as a long, heart-felt sigh escaped her. She plopped down on a wrought iron bench and let the smoothing sounds of early evening wash over her. The lone song of a nightingale, the distant rumble of carriage wheels on the cobblestone streets, the shouts of the grooms and neighing of horses coming from the mews.

The squeak of the back gate being opened.

Jossie peered through the growing darkness, expecting to see one of her aunt's servants. Instead, it was Adrian's tall figure walking purposefully toward her. With her heart hammering against her chest, she rose and hurried down the few flagstone steps to the gravel path to meet him.

It might have been a trick of the moonlight, but his usual cold, unreadable countenance appeared wretched, his piercing gaze dismal. Could he have missed her as much as she'd missed him?

"My lord, what are you doing here?" she asked breathlessly.

He halted a half dozen steps from her, and drew in an audible breath.

Chapter 25

Bloody hell, what was he doing here?

After bidding Jossie farewell, Adrian had returned to his townhouse where he'd spent most of his time holed up in his study since killing Carew, drinking heavily before venturing out to make the rounds of various gambling hells. Absurdly, despite his reckless playing, he managed to win a sizable bankroll. He'd return home in the small morning hours, then awoke late the next day to hear Paddison rebuking his nightly inebriation, as only a long trusted and valued batman could get away doing.

Last night, his restlessness led him to Willa Dunlap's brothel, where he'd drunk too much and rudely ignored Lisette. Finally, he stumbled out to the street and walked to White's, where he proceeded to work his way through most of a bottle of brandy before hitting another gaming hell.

This morning, when handing Adrian a tumbler containing Paddison's vile concoction that helped alleviate the excruciating pain in his skull, the former army sergeant began, "None of my affair—"

"That's right, so stubble it," Adrian warned with a menacing glare as his head pounded like cannon discharges.

Ignoring his lordship's warning, Paddison continued. "Seems you've a troubled soul, my lord. Only one way to cure it." The manservant waited a moment before explaining, "You need to confront what's bothering you. Come up with a campaign to conquer it."

With a speculative gleam, Adrian eyed his trusted batman for a long moment and drawled, "Not so easy. Means I'd have to quit working as an agent for the Crown."

"Not sure about that, though you'd have to quit the nightly visits to the gaming hells, stay out of the rookeries, become more respectable." Paddison shrugged. "Never known you to turn lily-livered before a battle, my lord." Quickly retrieving the empty tumbler from Adrian's raised hand before it was thrown at his pate, Paddison left the room, closing the door softly behind him.

For the remainder of the day, Adrian wrestled with himself. He knew Jossie was too good for the likes of him. She was light, he was dark. She was honest and truthful, well most of the time, he was a consummate liar. She was an innocent, he was a debauched scoundrel, who'd killed his man more than once.

But he was drawn to her like a parched and withered soul to a desert oasis.

That evening, he met up with a few friends

at White's, played cards, and partook of a light repast before calling it an early night and setting out to walk home. His feet, however, took him in the direction of Mount Street where he turned at the mews and stopped at the rear gate of Lady Welbeck's townhouse. Going through the gate, he hadn't known what to expect—certainly not encountering his heart's desire, standing in a pool of moonlight in the manicured garden.

His eyes roamed over wavy dark curls piled loosely atop her head, her large eyes that looked more silver than grey in her heart-shaped face. The slender neck, her heavenly curves draped in a white crepe robe over a pale pink slip with frilly lace across the modest neckline of her gown that fell to satin slippers with silver clasps.

She was an angel, and he'd only defile her. He pivoted on his heel to leave.

"Wait!" she called out, stopping him. "Why are you here?"

He ran a hand distractedly through his hair and slowly turned back to her. "I don't know."

Jossie shook her head. "You confuse me."

He drank in her luminous eyes, her slender figure, luscious curls, and a hunger for her surged from his very soul. "I confuse myself."

A small smile lifted her lips. "Do you know, I believe you might like me?"

Like her—hell, he wanted her in his arms, his bed. He wanted to possess her, every bit of her, now and forever. Never had a female so consumed his thoughts, haunted his dreams. He continued to stare at her, devouring every inch of her.

When a mischievous twinkle lit her eyes, he knew a moment of apprehension—one of the few he'd ever experienced in his sordid life.

"I accept your proposal," she said, her smile turning flirty.

"Beg pardon." Puzzled, he shook his head. "I've made no offer."

She slanted her head to one side. "Didn't you?"

She was adorable as a kitten, yet at the same time he saw the bewitching vixen. He drew back, suddenly realizing that this diminutive woman had the power to crush him. Of course, there were worst ways to die, he mused completely mesmerized by her.

Accepting his fate, he chuckled softly and stepped closer. "Have you no shame, Lady Jocelyn?"

"None," she admitted unabashedly, her smile even broader.

He pressed his lips together and grew serious. "I'm not a nice man, Jossie."

"Oh?" Her smile faded.

"I've lived my life as I wanted—uncaring about my fellow man . . . or woman," he confessed.

"Perhaps," she acquiesced. "But I think you've developed those, er, bad habits as means to defend your country."

"My work has taken on many aspects," he conceded.

"Even now?" Her hand made a gesture taking in the whole of the garden. "Is this part of your work?"

"No."

Tentatively, she inched closer. "Will you marry me, Adrian?"

His breathing hitched at the pleading note in her voice, though he remained silent, fearful he might yet hurt her.

Her eyes grew wider. "I'm offering you my heart." She bit her lower lip. "Please, do not stomp on it."

His own heart constricted painfully at the thought of losing her. He wanted nothing more than to accept her love. His chuckle held an agonized note. "Do you know the man I am?"

"Yes, I believe I do." She stepped to within inches of him, and he hungrily inhaled her lavender scent. "Do you know the woman I am?"

"Yes," he growled and reached for her, gathering her possessively in his arms. "A demanding, irritating, disobedient and utterly enchanting minx."

Her smile returned as she asked softly, "Does this mean you accept my proposal?"

He stared intently into her eyes and reiterated, "Your soul is untouched by evil, Jossie, while I'm a scoundrel of the worst sort, completely unworthy of you."

Her lips quivered with a tremulous smile. "I ask you again, Adrian George Hylton, Viscount Stangate, will you do me the honor of becoming my husband?"

"Bloody hell," he swore under his breath. Gazing at the love illuminated in her eyes by the moonlight, a moment of panic seized him before he remembered the agony, the utter desolation he'd experienced maintaining his distance from her over the past two weeks. "Forgive me, Jossie, but I can't live without you. I want to make a home with you, make you the mother of my children. So, yes." He ruthlessly possessed her lips with his as his hands roamed her back, pulling her closer to his body, reveling in her softness.

When he allowed her to come up for air, she squeaked, "Yes?"

"Yes." He kissed her again more tenderly before picking her up and carrying her to a stone bench where he sat with her snuggly in his arms on his lap. "We'll marry tomorrow by special license." He gave her a quizzical smile. "I'm not a patient man, Jossie. Were you hoping for a big wedding in St. George's Church?"

"No, not really," she giggled, then pulled back slightly. "There's something else, Adrian. I'll not share you with another woman . . . a mistress or anyone else."

He pulled her head against his shoulder. "My darling girl, you need never worry about me straying. You own me, Jossie, heart and soul. On that you have my word," he said with a wicked grim before he proceeded to show her just how much of him she possessed.

Thank you for purchasing *Lady Jocelyn Courts Blackmail*. If you have enjoyed this book, you may like to leave a review on Amazon or Goodreads to help other readers find it. Or visit my webpage at:

http://margaretbennett.net/

Or you can look for me on Facebook, Twitter, and Instagram.

Thank you,

Margaret Bennett

ABOUT THE AUTHOR

Margaret Bennett has lived most of her life in Norfolk, VA, married to a retired naval officer. Professionally, she has a diversified background with a Master's in Education from the University of Virginia and has taught middle and senior high school students for over twenty years, with nine years in alternative education for at-risk students. She started writing Regency romance stories as a hobby and now writes full time as her second career in beautiful Port Royal, SC.

LADY JOCELYN COURTS BLACKMAIL